"You?" Elodie gasped, heat flooding into her cheeks and other places in her body she didn't want to think about right now.

Lincoln Lancaster rose from his chair with leonine grace, his expression set in its customary cynical lines—the arch of one ink-black brow over his intelligent bluey-green gaze, the tilt of his sensual mouth that was not quite a smile. His black hair was brushed back from his high forehead in loose waves that looked like they had last been casually combed by his fingers. He was dressed in a three-piece suit that hugged his athletic frame, emphasizing the broadness of his shoulders, the taut trimness of his chest, flat abdomen and lean hips. He was the epitome of a successful man in his prime. Potent, powerful, persuasive. He got what he wanted, when he wanted, how he wanted.

"You're looking good, Elodie." His voice rolled over her as smoothly and lazily as his gaze, the deep sexy rumble so familiar it triggered a host of memories she had fought for seven years to erase.

The Scandalous Campbell Sisters

It started with a switch!

Twins Elspeth and Elodie Campbell may be identical, but looks aside, they couldn't be *more* different. So superconfident Elodie's idea that they switch places—at a society wedding no less!— has shy Elspeth on edge. Library archivist Elspeth would do anything for Elodie... But standing in for her supermodel sister? It's a recipe for disaster— surely! Add in a Scottish tycoon and an ex-fiancé... Well, life is about to get complicated for Elspeth and Elodie!

Meet the Campbell sisters in...
Elspeth and Mack's story
Shy Innocent in the Spotlight

Discover Elodie and Lincoln's story
A Contract for His Runaway Bride

Both available now!

Melanie Milburne

—

A CONTRACT FOR
HIS RUNAWAY BRIDE

HARLEQUIN

PRESENTS

Recycling programs
for this product may
not exist in your area.

ISBN-13: 978-1-335-56822-9

A Contract for His Runaway Bride

Copyright © 2021 by Melanie Milburne

Harlequin Enterprises ULC
22 Adelaide St. West, 40th Floor
Toronto, Ontario M5H 4E3, Canada
www.Harlequin.com

Printed in U.S.A.

Melanie Milburne read her first Harlequin novel at the age of seventeen, in between studying for her final exams. After completing a master's degree in education, she decided to write a novel, and thus her career as a romance author was born. Melanie is an ambassador for the Australian Childhood Foundation and a keen dog lover and trainer. She enjoys long walks in the Tasmanian bush. In 2015 Melanie won the HOLT Medallion, a prestigious award honoring outstanding literary talent.

Books by Melanie Milburne

Harlequin Presents

The Billion-Dollar Bride Hunt

The Scandalous Campbell Sisters

Shy Innocent in the Spotlight

Once Upon a Temptation

His Innocent's Passionate Awakening

Secret Heirs of Billionaires

Cinderella's Scandalous Secret

Wanted: A Billionaire

One Night on the Virgin's Terms
Breaking the Playboy's Rules
One Hot New York Night

Visit the Author Profile page at Harlequin.com for more titles.

To Denise Florence Monks. You were not just our help in the house (and in the garden and with house-sitting) but our help and support during some very difficult times. I will always treasure my memories of you. Your love and compassion for our family, our pets and even our friends was amazing. Even right to the end, you were thinking of others. Rest in peace.

CHAPTER ONE

ELODIE CAMPBELL GLANCED at her designer watch and muttered a colourful curse. The one time in her life when she was bang on time for an appointment and she was kept waiting. Who was this guy who thought it was okay to leave her out here with her nerves ripping her stomach to shreds?

This meeting was her last chance for financial backing.

It had to go ahead.

To fill the time—and to settle her anxiety—she'd glanced through the artfully splayed glossy magazines five times. One of which featured a spread of her on a photo shoot in Dubai. Then she'd consumed two expertly brewed black coffees. Maybe the second coffee hadn't been such a good idea. Restless at the best of times, now she was so fidgety she wanted to pace the floor...or punch something.

She crossed one leg over the other and kicked her top foot up and down in time with the tick-tock of the second hand on the clock above the receptionist's desk.

The clock went around another eight and a half minutes and Elodie was close to screaming. Not just a scream of frustration but one that was so loud it would shatter the windows of the swish-looking office tower. Normally people had to wait for her. Her identical twin, Elspeth, had inherited the punctuality gene. Elodie had got the chronically late one.

The longer she waited, the worse her anxiety spiked. What if this meeting turned out like the last? Her options were running out—especially since the recent scandal attached to her name. Her previous financial backer had pulled out once he'd heard about her role in sabotaging a society wedding. Urgh. What was it with her and scandals? If she couldn't secure financial backing, how could she leave her lingerie modelling career behind? She was tired of playing on her looks. She wanted to prove she had more than a good body. She wanted to design her own label of evening wear, but she needed an investor in her business to get it off the ground.

Another five minutes crawled past like a snail on crutches.

Elodie blew out a breath and sprang up from the sofa in the plush reception area on the top level of the London office tower. She strode over to the smartly dressed receptionist with a smile so forced it made her face ache. 'Could you give me an update on when Mr Smith will be available?'

The receptionist's answering smile was polite but formal. 'I apologise for the delay. He'll be with you shortly.'

'Look, my appointment was—'

'I understand, Ms Campbell. But he's a very busy man. He's made a special gap in his diary for you. He's not usually so accommodating. You must've made a big impression on him.'

'I haven't even met him. All I know is, I was instructed to be here close to thirty minutes ago for a meeting with a Mr Smith to discuss finance. I've been given no other details.'

The receptionist glanced at the intercom console where a small green light was flashing. She looked up again at Elodie with the same polite smile. 'Thank you for being so patient. Mr…erm… Smith will see you now. Please go through. It's the third door on the right. The corner office.'

The corner office boded well—that meant he was the head honcho. The big bucks began and stopped with him. Elodie went to the door and took a deep calming breath, but it did nothing to settle the frenzy of flick knives in her stomach. She gave the door a quick rap with her knuckles.

Please, please, please let me be successful this time.

'Come.'

Her hand paused on the doorknob, her mind whirling in ice-cold panic. Something about the deep timbre of that voice sent a shiver scuttling over her scalp like a small claw-footed creature. Elodie ran the tip of her tongue over her suddenly carpet-dry lips, her throat so tight she couldn't swallow. Surely her nerves were getting the better of her? The man she was meeting was a Mr Smith. But how could this Mr Smith sound so like her ex-fiancé? Scarily like him.

She turned the doorknob and pushed the door open, her gaze immediately fixing on the tall dark-haired man behind the large desk.

'You?' Elodie gasped, heat flooding into her cheeks and other places in her body she didn't want to think about right now.

Lincoln Lancaster rose from his chair with leonine grace, his expression set in its customary cynical lines—the arch of one ink-black brow over his intelligent bluey-green gaze, the tilt of his sensual mouth that was not quite a smile. His black hair was brushed back from his high forehead in loose waves that looked as if they had last been combed by his fingers. He was dressed in a three-piece suit that hugged his athletic frame, emphasising the broadness of his shoulders, the taut trimness of his chest, flat abdomen and lean hips. He was the epitome of a successful a man in his prime. Potent, powerful, persuasive. He got what he wanted, when he wanted, how he wanted.

'You're looking good, Elodie.'

His voice rolled over her as smoothly and lazily as his gaze, the deep, sexy rumble so familiar it triggered a host of memories she had fought for seven years to erase. Memories in her flesh that were triggered by being in his presence. Erotic memories that made her hyper-aware of his every breath, his every glance, his every movement.

Elodie shut the door behind her with a definitive click. She clenched her right hand around her slim-line purse and her other hand into a tight fist and stalked towards his desk. 'How dare you lie to me to get me here? You know I'd never willingly be in the same room as you.'

His eyes shone with amusement, which only fuelled her anger like a naked flame on tinder. 'You answered your own question. I wanted to meet with you and this seemed the only way to do it.'

'*Mr Smith?*' She made a scoffing noise. 'Couldn't you be a little more original than that? And why not meet me at your Kensington office?'

'In another life, Smith could well have been my name.'

There was a cryptic quality to his tone and a flicker of something in his expression that piqued her interest.

'I'm using this office for a few weeks while my other premises are being renovated.' He waved a hand at the plush chair in front of his desk. 'Take a seat. We have things to discuss.'

Elodie remained standing, her fists so tightly balled she could feel her fingernails cutting half-moons into the skin of her palm and the soft leather of her purse. 'I have nothing to discuss with you. You've no right to waste my valuable time by luring me here under false pretences.'

'Sit.' His one-word command was as sharp and implacable as the steely *don't-mess-with-me* glint in his eyes.

Elodie raised her chin, a frisson skittering over her flesh at the combative energy firing between them like high-voltage electricity. Fighting with Lincoln had formed a large part of their previous relationship. Their strong wills had often clashed and their passionate fights had nearly always been resolved in bed. The thought of *this* fight ending that way made her heart race and her pulse skyrocket.

'Just try and make me.'

She injected her tone with ice-cold disdain to counter the fiery heat pooling between her legs. Only Lincoln Lancaster could have this effect on her, and it made her furious to think he still had the power to make her feel things she didn't want to feel. Dangerous feelings. Overwhelming feelings. Feelings she couldn't control.

One side of his mouth came up in a half-smile, and the slow burn of his gaze sent tingles cascading down the length of her spine to pool in a ball of molten heat in her core.

'Tempting as that is, right now, I want to discuss a proposal with you.'

'A proposal?' She unclenched her fists and gave a bark of scathing laughter. 'There's nothing you could ever propose to me that I would find irresistible.'

There was a long beat of silence. A silence so weighted, so intense, it sent goosebumps popping up along the skin of her arms.

His unreadable eyes held hers in a lock that made her blood tick with excitement. It was an excitement she wished she could quell, but it seemed her body had a mind of its own when it came to Lincoln.

And somehow, she suspected he knew it.

Lincoln came around to perch on the corner of his desk, close enough to her for her to catch a tantalising whiff of his aftershave. The citrus notes were fresh and clean, the base notes a little more complex, reminding her of the rich, earthy scent of a densely wooded forest after rain. His eyes were an unusual mix of green and blue—a bottomless ocean with flashes of kelp and green sea glass swirling in their unreachable depths. She couldn't drag her eyes away from the dark shadow of regrowth peppering his jaw. How many times had she run her fingers over that prickly stubble? How many times had she felt its sexy rasp on the sensitive skin of her inner thighs?

Her gaze drifted to his mouth and her stomach bottomed out. Suddenly she found it hard to breathe. Those sensually curved lips had explored every inch of her body, stirred her into cataclysmic pleasure time and time again. She had never had a more exciting lover than Lincoln Lancaster. His touch had set fire to her body, making it erupt into roaring flames of need only he could assuage. Every lover since—not that there had been many—had been a bitter disappointment. It was as if Lincoln had ruined her for anyone else. No one could ignite her flesh like he had. No one could make her feel the things he made her feel. It seemed her body was programmed to respond to him and him alone.

'How about we start again?' His voice had a disarmingly gentle note, but his gaze was still unwavering on hers. 'You're looking good, Elodie.'

The pitch of his voice went down half a semitone

to a deep burr that put her resolve to resist him in Critical Care. He was impossible to resist when he laid on the charm.

Elodie swallowed the choking lump of her pride, intrigued by his change of tactic. Intrigued by why he had set up this meeting under a false name and in a high-rise office tower that was on the other side of town from his London base. Intrigued to find out exactly what he was proposing. Office renovations aside, surely he could have contacted her without the need for pretence?

'Thank you.' She glanced behind her to locate the chair and sat—not because she wanted to do as he had commanded earlier, but because right then her legs were feeling decidedly unsteady. She positioned her leather purse on her lap, her fingers absently fidgeting with the silver clasp. 'You said you had something to discuss with me? A proposal?'

Lincoln rose from his perch on the edge of the desk and went back to sit in his office chair. He rolled the chair forward and then rested one of his forearms on the desk. His other hand reached for a sheaf of papers.

'A business proposal.' His gleaming eyes met hers and he added, 'You weren't expecting any other type of proposal, were you?'

Elodie schooled her features into cool impassivity. 'I can't imagine you'd be interested in repeating past mistakes.'

An inscrutable smile tilted one side of his mouth. 'I hear you're interested in some financial backing for your own evening wear label.' He drummed his fingers on the paperwork beneath his hand. 'Are you interested in hearing my terms?'

Elodie ran the tip of her tongue over her lips, aware of another moth-like flicker of excitement in her blood. Could this be her chance to fulfil her dream at last? She had never aspired to be a lingerie model, but she had played the role with aplomb. *Smart*, *successful*, *sassy*, *sophisticated* and *sexy* were the five words to describe her brand. A brand she had never intended adopting in the first place but had somehow drifted into. Lincoln was offering her an escape route—but he'd mentioned terms. What would they be? Dared she even ask? He was one of the most successful self-made businessmen in the country. He turned around ailing businesses within a year or two for a sizeable profit. Did he see her venture as a sure bet?

'You want to finance me? But…but why?'

He shrugged one broad shoulder, his expression as unreadable as a mask. 'I never allow emotions to get in the way of a good business deal.'

Did that mean he was confident she could succeed? How strange that he of all people believed in her potential. 'You think I can be successful?'

His gaze was suddenly laser-pointer-direct. 'Do you?'

'I…' Elodie chewed at the inside of her mouth and lowered her gaze from the penetrating heat of his. 'I think so.'

'Not good enough. You have to believe in yourself or no one else will.'

The chiding edge to his tone made her straighten her back in her chair. She brought her gaze back to his. 'I do believe in myself. I've wanted to get out of modelling for a while now. I want to prove I have more to offer the world than my looks.'

'A wishbone and a backbone are two different things. How much do you want it?'

She disguised a tiny swallow. 'More than anything.'

One dark eyebrow lifted over his mercurial gaze. 'Are you sure about that?'

Elodie lifted her chin, locking her gaze on his. 'Positive.'

Lincoln pushed the paperwork across the desk to her. 'Good. Because in here are my terms. You can read them at your leisure, but I can summarise them for you here and now if you like.'

Elodie laid her purse on the floor and took the sheaf of documents, but she knew it would take her ages to read through it carefully due to her dyslexia. And so did he. Not that he had ever made an issue of her learning problems in the past—if anything he had been surprisingly accommodating and understanding. It was another way he had charmed her into thinking he cared about her for more than her looks—more fool her.

'Please do.'

He leaned back in his chair, one forearm still resting on his desk. His posture was casual—almost too casual, given the searing intensity of his gaze. 'I'll put forward the necessary finance for you to launch your label.'

He named a sum that made her perfectly groomed eyebrows almost fly off her face. She knew he was wealthy, but surely that was a ridiculous amount of money to be offering her—especially given the way their relationship had ended.

Elodie rapid-blinked, her heart thumping like a hard fist against her ribcage. *Ba-boom. Ba-boom. Ba-boom.* 'But why would you want to do that?'

He held up a hand like a stop sign, his expression difficult to read. 'Allow me to state my terms without interruption.' He lowered his hand to the desk and continued. 'The money is yours if you'll agree to be my wife for six months.'

Elodie stared at him with her mind reeling, her pulse racing, her stomach freefalling. *His wife?* Was he joking? Was this some sort of candid camera prank? And why only six months? Wasn't a marriage meant to be for ever?

The money was more than enough to launch her label. Along with her own savings, the money would mean she would be able employ the necessary staff to help her achieve her dream. But to become his wife? To live with him, sleep with him, spend every day with him…? *Risk the chance of falling in love with him?*

She had come perilously close to losing herself in their relationship in the past.

Could she risk the same happening again?

Elodie narrowed her eyes and leaned forward to

place the papers back on his desk. 'Is this some kind of joke?'

Lincoln picked up a gold cartridge pen and rocked it back and forth between two of his long, tanned fingers. 'It's no joke.'

His gaze remained marksman-steady and it sent a shiver of reaction through her body. Could he see how much his presence unsettled her? Could he sense the magnetic power he still had over her? A power she fought to resist with every cell of her body...

She swallowed and tried not to stare at his fingers—tried not to recall how those fingers felt when they touched her, excited her, pleasured her. She forced her gaze back to his, her heart thumping so loudly she was surprised he couldn't hear it. 'You know I can't do that.'

He tossed the pen to one side and it rolled up against a glass paperweight with a soft tinkle that seemed overly loud in the silence. 'Your call. But I should warn you this offer is only open for twenty-four hours. After that, it's off the table and won't be repeated.'

Elodie rose from her chair in one agitated movement, her arms going around her middle. She wanted to slap him for being so arrogant as to think she would accept. She wanted to grab him by the front of his shirt and...and...press her mouth to... *No.* She slammed the brakes on her wayward thoughts. She did *not* want to go anywhere near his sensual mouth.

'I can't believe you're doing this. What can you possibly hope to achieve?'

'I need a wife for the period of six months. It's as simple as that.'

She curled her top lip. 'I'm sure you have plenty of willing candidates to choose from.'

'Ah, but I want you.'

The silky smoothness of his tone threatened to put her willpower on life support, but Elodie raised her chin at a defiant angle, determined to hold her ground for as long as she could.

'What about the woman I saw you with last time we ran in to each other? She looked like she was madly in love with you. I was surprised you could still breathe with her arms clasped around your neck like that.'

His smile was indolent, his eyes glinting. 'She was in love with me. And that's why she's not suitable for this position.'

Elodie frowned so hard even a hefty shot of Botox wouldn't have prevented her wrinkling her brow. 'I don't understand… Are you saying you don't want—?'

'I can hardly want someone to be in love with me if I only want them to be my wife for six months.'

Elodie stood behind the chair and grasped the back with both hands. Something low and deep in her belly was doing somersaults. Rapid somersaults that made her intimate muscles twitch in memory of his rock-hard presence.

'Why only six months?'

He rose from the desk and slipped off his jacket, hanging it on the back of his chair. His movements were methodical, precise, as if he were mentally preparing a speech. His expression was cast in lines of gravitas she was not used to seeing on his face.

'My mother is terminally ill. She wants to see me settled before she dies.'

Elodie's frown deepened to one of confusion. 'Your mother? But you told me your mother died a couple of months before we met.'

His lips moved in a grim smile—a stiff movement of his lips that had nothing to do with what a smile was meant to be. 'That was my adoptive mother. I only met my biological mother a couple of years ago.'

Her eyes widened and she became aware of a sharp pain underneath her heart. A burrowing pain that almost took her breath away. He was adopted? Why had he never mentioned it? She knew every inch of his body, knew how he took his coffee, what brand of suit he preferred, knew his taste in literature and film, knew how he looked when he came… But he had never told her one of the most important things about himself.

'You never told me you were adopted. Did you know when we were—?'

'I always knew I was adopted.'

'But you chose not to tell me, the woman you asked to be your wife?'

Anger laced her tone and the pain in her chest burrowed a little deeper, a little harder, as if working its way towards her backbone like a silent drill. Why hadn't he told her something as important as that? It only confirmed the suspicions she'd had all along— he hadn't been in love with her. He'd been attracted to her, but love hadn't come into it at all. He had chosen her for her looks, not for *her*.

And wasn't that the miserable story of her life?

CHAPTER TWO

'BUT YOU CHOSE *not* to be my wife, remember?' Lincoln said, with an edge of bitterness that even after all these years he couldn't quite quell. Nor did he want to. His bitterness had fuelled the phenomenal success he'd achieved in the seven years since Elodie Campbell had left him standing at the altar.

He would never admit it to her, but she had actually done him a favour by jilting him. It had galvanised him, motivated him to build an empire that rivalled some of the largest in England, if not the world. He had quadrupled his income, built his assets into an enviable portfolio that gave him the sort of security most people only dreamed about. Aiming for success had always been his passion, a driving force in his personality, but her rejection had amped up his drive to a whole new level. Everything he touched turned to gleaming gold. He *made* it do so. Nothing stood in his way when he was on a mission to achieve a goal.

Nothing and no one.

But seeing her again stirred other feelings in him that were equally difficult to ignore. Feelings he had squashed, buried, disposed of with ruthless determination.

Her beauty had always been captivating. Her long wavy red-gold hair hung halfway down her back like a mermaid's. Her heart-shaped face with its aristocratic cheekbones, retroussé nose and uptilted bee-stung mouth gave her a haughty, untouchable air that had drawn him from the first moment he'd met her. Her body was slender, and yet her feminine curves made him ache to skim his hands over them as he'd used to do.

She was strong-willed and feisty, passionate and impulsive, and no one had ever excited him or stood up to him as much as her. He had never forgotten the thrill of arguing with her. A fight with her had not been just a fight—it had been a full-on war that always ended explosively in bed. He got hard just thinking about it.

No one had ever pushed back against him the way Elodie did.

And no one had ever humiliated him the way she had.

The business proposal he was offering now was his way of ruling a line underneath their relationship. If she accepted his terms he would be the one to end their relationship this time. He had loved her and lost her, and he would never give her, or indeed anyone, the power to make a fool of him again.

Elodie moved away from the chair she was holding on to and wrapped her arms around her middle. 'It seems my decision to jilt you was the right one.'

She threw him a glance so frosty he wished he hadn't taken off his jacket. 'How could you have withheld something so important from me?'

Lincoln shrugged one shoulder. 'It wasn't something I talked about to anyone.'

'But why? Were you ashamed of it? Were you upset at being relinquished as a baby?'

'I was neither ashamed nor upset.'

Lincoln had known since he was old enough to understand the concept that he had been adopted. His adoptive parents had been loving and supportive parents and his childhood mostly happy. He had also known his younger brother and sister were his parents' biological children. But instead of feeling pushed aside and less important, he had been reassured by his parents that he was the reason they had been able to have their own biological children. That their love and nurturing of him had unlocked their unexplained infertility.

'But while we're on the subject of withholding information—why did you choose to run away on our wedding day instead of talking to me about your concerns? You've never adequately explained your actions, and nor have you apologised to me face to face.'

Twin circles of colour bloomed in her cheeks and her gaze slipped out of reach of his. 'I'm sorry if you were embarrassed. I—I just couldn't go through with it.'

Lincoln let out a stiff curse. 'The least you could have done is told me to my face. It would have saved a lot of unnecessary expense.'

'Oh, so it was the money angle that upset you the most?' Her voice had a cutting edge, her blue gaze flashing fire. 'You were the one who wanted a big wedding and insisted on paying for everything.'

'Only because I didn't want to put that sort of load on your mother. I knew your father wouldn't help out.'

Elodie bent down to pick up her purse off the floor near her chair, her long glossy hair momentarily hiding her expression. She straightened and shook her hair back over her shoulders. 'I have to go.'

He ached to run those silken strands through his fingers, to lift handfuls of her fragrant hair to his nose and breathe in her exotic scent. It had taken him months to get rid of the smell of her perfume in his house, even though he had instructed his house-keeper to remove every trace of Elodie. Every room had seemed to hold a hint of her distinctive scent, lingering there to silently mock him.

Look what happens when you fall in love. You are left with nothing but memories to taunt you.

'I want your answer by five p.m. tomorrow.'

Her defiant gaze met his and a lightning bolt of lust slammed into his groin. 'I gave you my answer. It's an emphatic, don't-embarrass-yourself-by-asking--me-again *no*.'

Lincoln leaned his hip against the corner of his desk and folded his arms across his chest. He hadn't expected her to say yes at the first meeting. It wasn't in her nature to do anything without a fight and, frankly, he admired that about her. But seeing her again had proved to him she wasn't immune to him, and that gave him the assurance that she would eventually agree to his terms.

That he wasn't immune to her was an issue he would have to address at some point. He would not allow her the same sensual power she'd had over him in the past. The sensual power that had made him propose marriage within a couple of months of meeting her. The stunning physicality of their relationship had blindsided him to the reality of her using him, rather than loving him. She had said the words but she had still bolted. That was not love—that was betrayal of the highest order. And he would not allow it to happen again.

'Don't let your emotions get in the way. I can help you achieve your dream. It can be a win-win for both of us.'

'Why are you doing this?'

'I told you—I need a temporary wife.'

'But marrying someone you don't love and who doesn't love you is hardly honouring your biological mother in the final weeks or months of her life. Won't she be able to tell it's not a love match?'

'Nina Smith knows you jilted me seven years ago. She's a hopeless romantic who believes I'll never be happy until we get back together. She disapproves of my playboy lifestyle and wants to see me settled before she passes on.' His mouth stretched into a cynical smile and he added, 'You were good at pretending to love me in the past. I'm sure you'll do an excellent job this time around—especially given the amount of money I'd be paying you.'

Her lips were tightly compressed. 'If—and it's a big if—if I accept your offer, I won't sleep with you.'

Lincoln pushed himself away from his desk and picked up the sheaf of papers, held them out to her. 'You won't be required to. It's written in the contract. You'll find it on page three.'

She took the papers from him as if he was handing her a dangerous animal. She laid them on the desk and began to read painstakingly through the pages. Then her eyes rounded and she lifted her gaze back to his. 'A paper marriage?'

Lincoln smiled a victor's smile. 'Won't that be fun?'

Later, Elodie would barely recall leaving Lincoln's office. She'd only vaguely remember stalking past the smartly dressed receptionist and getting into the lift. Her mind was numb all the way down to the ground floor. It was still barely functioning by the time she met her twin, Elspeth, for coffee in Notting Hill half an hour later.

'I was about to give up on you,' Elspeth said as soon as Elodie dropped into the chair opposite with a thump. 'Hey, are you okay? You look a little flustered. What's wrong?'

'Sorry I'm so late.' Elodie placed her purse on the table. 'My meeting ran over time.'

'How did it go?'

Elodie was reluctant to share every detail of the meeting with her twin, even though they were close. It was still too raw.

Lincoln didn't want to sleep with her. It was to be a paper marriage.

The one thing they had got right about their relationship was sex. They'd been dynamite together. No one could ever say there had been something wrong with their sex life. They'd been more than compatible. Why, then, did he want a hands-off arrangement? Did it mean he would have someone else on the side? That she would be humiliated by him conducting numerous affairs under her nose?

'It was…interesting.'

Elspeth leaned forward, her eyes bright. 'So, what was this Mr Smith like? Was he keen to back your label?'

'He was very keen.'

'So why are you frowning?'

Elodie let out a sigh and poured herself a glass of water from the bottle on the table. 'Mr Smith is an alias.' She glanced at her twin's intrigued expression and added, 'It was Lincoln.'

Elspeth's eyebrows shot up. 'Lincoln?'

'Yup. He wants to back my label.'

'Wow.' Elspeth sat back in her chair, her expression puzzled. 'Why would he want to do that?'

Elodie gave her a look. 'Because he wants something in exchange.'

She couldn't keep this to herself any longer. Raw as it still was, she had to talk it through with someone, and who better than her twin?

'Me.'

Elspeth's eyes rounded to the size of the saucer

under her coffee cup. 'He wants you back? Oh, how romantic. I always thought he still had feelings for you, and—'

Elodie pursed her lips and shifted them from side to side. 'Not exactly. He wants me to marry him for six months. A paper marriage.'

Elspeth's mouth dropped open. 'A paper marriage? You mean no sleeping together? Seriously? What did you say?'

'I said no.'

'No?'

Elodie frowned. 'Why are you looking at me like that? Do you think I should agree to such a preposterous proposal?'

'I guess if you said yes it would give you both time to sort out your differences. There's clearly unfinished business between you. And if he's going to finance your label—well, surely that's a bonus?'

Elodie leaned her elbows on the table and, bending forward, rested her forehead on her splayed fingertips. 'Argh! I hate that man *so* much. I thought I knew him so well, and yet he kept one of the most important things about himself from me.'

She lifted her head out of her hands and filled her twin in on the circumstances behind Lincoln's proposal.

'I knew I was right to jilt him. This proves it. He didn't allow me to know him. The *real* him.'

Elspeth stroked a gentle hand over Elodie's wrist. 'If you can't bear the thought of accepting the money from him, then let Mack help you. He's happy to finance your label and—'

Elodie raised her face from her hands and sat up straighter in her chair. The thought had crossed her mind before, but she knew she could never ask her twin's fiancé for financial help. She wanted to keep her financial affairs separate and under her control.

'No. I can't accept money from Mack. I have twenty-four hours before I have to give my final answer to Lincoln.' She drummed her fingers on the table for a moment, her thoughts going around on a hamster's wheel. 'You know, there could be a positive spin on this… Imagine the press exposure I'd get if I went back to Lincoln. Who doesn't love a romantic reunion story? The news of us getting back together would go viral. It would boost my profile enormously. Lincoln said it could be a win-win, but I didn't see how until just now.' She beamed at her twin. 'He thinks he has me under his control, but he's in for a big surprise.'

Elspeth chewed at her lower lip, her face etched in lines of concern. 'I hope you know what you're doing.'

Elodie tossed her hair back over her shoulders. 'I know exactly what I'm doing. And, what's more, I can't wait to do it.'

Elodie dressed carefully for her follow-up meeting with Lincoln. She wasn't vain, but she knew the good-looks fairy had been especially generous to her and her twin. And years of being in hair and make-up sessions had given her skills that rivalled some of the top professionals.

Her make-up highlighted the blue of her eyes and the updo of her hair showcased the slim length of her neck. She put on diamond droplet earrings—a gift from one of the lingerie designers. She slipped on an emerald-green designer dress gifted to her after a photo shoot. It came to just above her knee and had a deep cleavage.

She smoothed the close-fitting dress over her slim hips and turned from side to side in front of her full-length mirror. Lincoln might think he could keep her at arm's length, but she had a point to prove. A point to win. A score to settle. He might not have ever loved her, but he'd desired her with a ferocity she knew she could trigger in him again. She'd seen the way he'd looked at her, his scorching gaze running over her body, the way he'd kept glancing at her mouth.

She smiled at her reflection. 'Let's see how long you can keep your hands off me now, Lincoln Lancaster.'

Lincoln was reading through some paperwork in his home office when he caught sight of Elodie on the security camera screen on his desk. He dropped the pen he was holding and stared at her for a long moment, drinking in her feminine form like a badly dehydrated man might stare at a long, cool glass of water, hardly daring to believe it was real.

She was dressed in a stunning green dress that left little to the imagination—and he didn't need much imagination, because he remembered every sexy curve of her body. He had explored and tasted every inch of it, and spent many a night since their breakup aching to do so again. No one had ever worked him up as much as Elodie Campbell. And that irritated the hell out of him.

The desire to settle down had come upon him the moment he'd met her. At twenty-one, she'd been bright and funny and wildly entertaining. He'd been twenty-eight years old, and still reeling from the sudden death of his adoptive mother. Falling fast and hard for Elodie had made him long to recreate the secure family unit he had grown up with. And watching his father slide into a deep depression had only reinforced Lincoln's desire to settle down. He'd figured it would offer his dad some hope for the future—a beautiful daughter-in-law, grandkids at some point…

Elodie's energy and vitality had lifted him out of his own funk of grief and within a couple of months he'd found himself on bended knee with an expensive diamond ring in his hand. He had never been the impulsive, spur-of-the-moment type, but something about her bewitching personality had unlocked the armour around his heart.

It was a decision he had come to regret, and bitterly, but now he had the power to end their relationship—this time around on his terms.

The only thing he was grateful for was he had never actually told her he loved her out loud. He had shown it in a thousand ways, but saying the words had been difficult for him. Elodie, on the other hand, had professed to love him many times—which just showed how empty those three little words could be. They were cheap, and overused, and he had been fooled by them, but he would not allow himself to be taken in by them again.

Elodie used people to get where she wanted to go, and she had used him callously and deceptively. She had been a virtual unknown before her fling with him, but her career had taken off after she'd jilted him. She had ruthlessly used him to get the social exposure she'd craved. That was the thing that niggled at him the most—she had used *his* public humiliation to launch her career.

Now she needed him in her quest for a career-change and he was happy to help. More than happy to help. Because this time around he would call the shots. Each and every one of them. Or die trying.

Elodie shifted her weight from foot to foot, annoyed that Lincoln was keeping her waiting again. She knew he was home, for his top-model sports car was parked in the driveway and there were lights on in his Victorian mansion.

She pressed her finger on the bell once more and looked directly into the security camera positioned above the entrance. She considered waving, but then the stained-glass and glossy black arched double front doors suddenly opened automatically, and she stepped inside.

The doors whispered shut behind her with a barely audible click, somehow giving her a vague sense of being imprisoned. She shook off the sensation and straightened her shoulders. She wasn't one to be intimidated by anyone or anything—even if this house did hold some memories she wished she could forget. Disturbingly sexy memories that made her body feel hot all over.

'Hello?' Elodie's voice echoed eerily in the spacious foyer.

The floor was light-coloured Italian marble with grey flecks and the walls a chalk-white. From the high ceiling hung a large crystal chandelier, and a grand sweeping staircase with black balustrading wound its way to the upper floors. A walnut and brass inlaid drum table with curved pedestal legs was positioned in front of the staircase, and a cymbidium orchid in luscious full bloom was situated on top, with a selection of hardback wildlife and wilderness books.

On the other side of the foyer there was a large brass inlaid dresser with twin crystal lamps either side of a gold-framed mirror that made the area seem even more spacious. Another orchid was positioned between the lamps, and either side of the dresser were two dark grey velvet wing chairs, which gave a welcoming and balanced feel to the formal entrance.

The sound of a footfall on the staircase brought her gaze up and she watched as Lincoln came towards her. She was glad it was him and not his crotchety old housekeeper, who had never made her feel welcome in the past. Hopefully Mean Morag had long gone.

Lincoln was wearing casual latte-coloured chinos with a light blue open-necked casual shirt that made the blue in his eyes dominate the green. The shirt was rolled halfway up his strong tanned forearms, the rich dusting of masculine hair spreading from his arms to the backs of his hands and along each of his fingers reminding her of the potent male hormones surging through his body.

'I've been expecting you.'

His voice held a trace of amusement, and she wondered how long he had been watching her via the security camera.

'It took you long enough to open the door.' Elodie threw him a churlish look. 'I was freezing my butt off out there.'

His eyes ran over her outfit from head to toe, lingering a moment on the deep valley of her cleavage. 'Then maybe you should have worn a coat.'

And spoil the knock-his-socks-off effect? No way.

Elodie sent her gaze around the foyer once more. 'You've redecorated since I was here last.'

No doubt he'd gone to great expense to rid his house of every trace of her. She seemed to recall he'd had a fling with an interior designer a few years ago. One of many glamourous women he'd been seen out and about with in the seven years since their cancelled wedding. Lincoln could barely change his brand of toothpaste without the press commenting on it, which was why her decision to accept his proposal would be so lucrative and important for launching her label.

'What do you think?' he asked.

She gave an indifferent shrug. 'It's nice enough.'

Lincoln's smile was sardonic, making her wonder if he could read her mind. 'Would you like a drink?'

'Sure.'

He led the way to a grand sitting room off the foyer, which had three large windows on one side overlooking the formal garden. A large sofa and matching armchairs were positioned in the middle of the room on a luxurious rug that left a wide boundary of the parquet floor on show. The grand fireplace had a large mirror above the mantelpiece and another crystal chandelier hung from the ceiling. Lamps were tastefully situated between each of the three large windows, on antique tables, and there were fresh flowers on the round coffee table in front of the sofa and chairs.

Elodie plonked herself down on one of the chairs and crossed her legs, watching as Lincoln went to a cleverly hidden drinks cabinet complete with fridge on the wall further along from the fireplace. 'Have you still got the same housekeeper?'

'I have, actually.' Lincoln took out a bottle of champagne and set it on the top of the cabinet with two tall crystal flutes. 'Will that be a problem for you?'

Elodie inspected her nails rather than meet his gaze. 'Why should it be?'

He popped the cork on the champagne. 'I seem to recall you and Morag never quite hit it off.' He proceeded to pour dancing bubbles into the two glasses.

'That's because she didn't respect me. I was your partner...your fiancée. But behind your back she treated me like I was gold-digging trailer trash. It was one of the first things she said to me when I met her. "You're only after his money and fame".'

That she had benefited from that fame after their breakup was neither here nor there, in her mind. Elodie had not agreed to marry him for any other reason than she wanted to be with him. Because… Because she'd been a silly little fool back then, who'd thought lust equalled love.

A taut line formed around Lincoln's mouth, as if he recalled every heated argument they'd used to have over his housekeeper. 'Perhaps you didn't treat her with the respect she deserved.'

He came over with the two glasses of champagne, handing one to her. Elodie did everything she could to avoid touching his fingers as she took the glass, but in spite of her efforts a tingle shot up her arm when his fingers brushed hers.

'Or perhaps she always knew you weren't going to stick around.'

Elodie made a snorting noise and took a generous sip of her champagne. 'She was just plain rude to me. She should have retired years ago.'

'Elodie.' The was a heavy note of censure in his tone and a frown was carved deep into his forehead.

She gave a nonchalant shrug and took another sip of champagne. 'So, aren't you going to ask me what I've decided about your proposal?'

Lincoln sat opposite her on the large sofa and stretched one of his strongly muscled arms along the back. 'I already know what you've decided. You wouldn't be here if your answer was still a flat-out no.'

Elodie circled one of her ankles round and round, not sure she was comfortable with him being able to read her so well. 'I've thought it through and I agree with you. It can be win-win for both of us—especially with the on-paper-only clause.' She raised her glass in a mock toast, painting a sugar-sweet smile on her lips. 'I would never have accepted without that.'

Lincoln rose from the sofa and placed his champagne glass on the coffee table between them with a thud. He straightened and nailed her with his gaze. 'There are some ground rules we need to establish from the get-go. Just because we don't sleep with each other doesn't mean we sleep with anyone else during the duration of our marriage. Is that clear?'

Elodie raised her eyebrows and whistled through her teeth. 'My, oh, my… That's going to be harder for you than me, isn't it? Celibacy isn't quite your thing, as I recall. You had someone else in your bed within a week of our cancelled wedding.'

His jaw became granite-hard. 'And that rankled, did it?'

'Nope.' She injected her tone with insouciance. 'I didn't want you, so why would I be upset someone else did?'

His eyes bored into hers with the intensity of an industrial strength drill, but Elodie was determined not to look away first. The tension in the air was palpable. A vibrating, pulsating tension that travelled along the invisible waves of silence like an electric current.

'But you want me now.' A cynical smile slanted his mouth and his eyes glinted challengingly.

Elodie laughed and tipped back her head. She drained her champagne glass, then leaned forward to set it on the coffee table next to his. 'Actually, I think you've got that the wrong way around. It's you who wants me.'

'And you know this because…?'

Elodie rose from the sofa and sashayed over to where he was standing, driven by an irresistible and recklessly rebellious urge to make him eat his words. She stood right in front of him and, locking her gaze on his, slid her hands up his muscular chest to rest on the tops of his impossibly broad shoulders. She breathed in the intoxicating scent of him—the wood and citrus and salty male scent that sent her senses into a tailspin. His eyes were hooded, his expression inscrutable, but she could sense a palpable tension in him.

'I know this because of the way you look at me.' She ran her index finger down the straight blade of his nose. 'It's the way you've always looked at me. Like you want to lick every inch of my body.' She kept her voice husky and whisper-soft, her gaze sultry.

He drew in a breath and let it out in a jagged stream. 'I told you the rules.'

Elodie moved a little closer, so her breasts brushed against his chest. A wave of incendiary heat swept through her at the contact, making her inner core contract with longing. She lifted her finger to his lips, tracing the sensual shape with deliberate slowness. 'You know all about me and rules.'

Lincoln grasped her by the upper arms in a hold that hinted at the coiled tension in his body. His eyes were diamond-hard, his expression grimly determined. 'We're not doing this.' The words were bitten out through tight lips.

Elodie stood on tiptoe, which pressed her breasts even more firmly against his chest. Her mouth was so close to his she could feel the warm waft of his breath mingling intimately with hers. 'But we both want to, don't we?'

She brushed her lips against his firm ones but he didn't respond. Goaded by his intractability, she pressed her lips on his and then slowly stroked her tongue along the seam of his mouth. He smothered a groan-cum-curse deep in his throat and crushed his mouth to hers.

It was a kiss that contained so many things— unruly and fiery passion, frustration, and even a little anger. Elodie didn't care. All she wanted was his mouth on hers, working its old magic on her senses. His tongue entered her mouth with a commanding thrust so like the way he'd used to enter her body she almost came on the spot. The taste of him was so familiar it triggered a firestorm of lust in her flesh. She groaned against his lips, winding her arms around his neck, needing, wanting, aching to be closer to the hard ridge of his erection.

No one could turn her on like Lincoln. No one. His touch was so electric, his kiss so explosively passionate, she had no hope of resisting even if she'd wanted to.

But just as quickly as the kiss started it ended, as if a cord had suddenly been tugged out of an electric appliance.

Lincoln pulled away from her with a cynical smile. 'Not going to happen this time, baby.'

Elodie disguised her disappointment behind a cool smile. 'Let me guess—there's someone else? I hope you're not going to humiliate me by seeing her while you're married to me.'

'You're a fine one to accuse *me* of humiliation.' There was no mistaking the bitterness in his tone, or the rigid set of his jaw. 'I think you deserve the prize for that.'

Elodie wasn't proud of the way she had ended their relationship, but at the time it had seemed her only escape route. She had let things go too far without talking to Lincoln about her career plans and her worries over how their relationship would cope. How she would juggle being a wife with being a lingerie model.

He had said he wanted children at some point. Even his father had mentioned how much he was looking forward to grandchildren. But what would have happened to her career if she'd got pregnant sooner rather than later? At the age of twenty-one, having children wasn't even on her radar. And even now, at twenty-eight, she still hadn't heard a single peep from her biological clock. Her career was her focus. Her drive and ambition left no room for anything else.

'I understand how embarrassing it must have been for—'

'But it achieved what you wanted it to achieve, didn't it? You were a nobody until you got involved with me. Jilting me got you the press attention you always wanted, and you built your career off the back of it.'

Elodie stared at him speechlessly for a long moment, her mind whirling like clothes in a tumble dryer. He thought she had *used* him? That nothing about her involvement with him had been more than a tactical move to gain fame? That might be her plan now, but back then she *had* loved him. Truly loved him. Had told him so many times. Her feelings for him had been overwhelming—so much so they had contributed to her rash decision to jilt him.

She had sensed that if she married him, her career would never be a priority. Her priority would be him. His priority would never be her. To Lincoln, all she would have been was a trophy wife. He had never told her he loved her, and until the last moment she had been too star-struck by him to see that was a problem—an alarm bell she should have paid far more attention to. She had fooled herself into believing he was one of those men who wasn't comfortable with expressing his emotions. She had fooled herself into thinking he actually *felt* the emotions just because their lovemaking was so incredible.

But complete strangers could have incredible sex—love had nothing to do with it.

Elodie walked over to the drinks cabinet, where Lincoln had left the champagne bottle, and brought it over to refill her glass. She placed the bottle down on the coffee table and sent him a sideways glance. 'I find it highly amusing that you're accusing me of using you when all you wanted was for me to be a trophy wife, a bit of arm candy to show off to all your friends and business associates. You didn't love me.'

Lincoln compressed his mouth into a flat line. 'At least we're equal on that score. Love was never a part of our relationship.'

There—he had admitted it. He had never loved her. Elodie did everything in her power to disguise the pain his words evoked. But then she had always been good at masking her emotions, and if she couldn't mask them she ran away from them.

Growing up with a twin with a life-threatening nut allergy had taught her how to play down her panic, to keep cool under pressure, never to show the turmoil she was actually feeling at the thought of losing her sister. In a perverse kind of way, she had adopted a devil-may-care approach to life. And her rebellious streak had strengthened as her mother's overzealous attention had focussed more and more on her twin. Negative attention was better than no attention, and it was a pattern that had followed her through life.

'I'd like to know more about what you expect of me during our six months marriage,' she said, with no trace of the turmoil she was feeling. 'What are our living arrangements, for instance?'

Lincoln picked up his glass of barely touched champagne but didn't drink from it. 'We'll live together but have separate rooms.'

Elodie raised her brows. 'And what's your housekeeper going to think about that?'

Would she have to endure more rejection? More stinging little asides from the housekeeper about how she wasn't good enough for Lincoln and never would be? Words that had been reinforced by the rejection of her father and everyone else who had never believed in her and only seen value in her looks, not in her as a person.

'She'll think what I pay her to think.'

'You're not worried she might leak the truth about our relationship to the press?'

'No.'

Elodie twirled the contents of her champagne glass, her eyes still trained on his masklike expression. 'What about when either of us needs to travel for work? Are you going to come with me and expect me to come with you?'

'We'll be together as much as possible, when work and other commitments allow.'

Elodie wondered what his 'other commitments' might be. For a man with such a healthy and robust sexual appetite, she couldn't imagine him taking on celibacy for six days, let alone six months. And how would she cope with living with him in close proximity? Especially given their passionate history? The sexual chemistry between them was ever-present. It was like a current in the air…a humming, buzzing frequency that sent tingles all over her flesh.

She took a sip of her champagne and then asked, 'Are we having a big wedding? I mean, it would look more romantic and convincing if we—'

'No.' The word was delivered bluntly. 'We'll be married in a register office with only two witnesses.'

'No press?'

His gaze was steely. Impenetrable. 'I'll make an announcement once we are officially married.'

'And when will that be?'

'Tomorrow.'

Elodie widened her eyes, felt her heart slipping sideways in her chest. 'That soon? Don't you have to get a license and stuff?'

'Already done.'

How had he been so confident of her agreeing to his proposal? Did he think she still had feelings for him? Feelings he could take advantage of to suit his own ends? But her feelings for him were in deep freeze. She had locked her heart in a block of ice that was resistant to his charm. She could not afford to fall for him again.

'You were so sure I'd say yes?'

'I've learned that nothing is ever a certainty with you, but let's say I was quietly confident.'

'You do know I'm only doing it for the money, don't you?'

His half-smile was cynical. 'But of course.'

Elodie put her glass down and tucked a loose

strand of hair behind her ear. 'And when do I get to meet your mother?'

'The following day. We'll fly to Spain and spend a couple of days there.'

'She lives in Spain? Is she Spanish, or—?'

'English. But she enjoys the warmer climate there. It's where she wants to spend the rest of her days.'

'What if it doesn't suit me to fly to Spain?' Elodie asked, not sure she wanted to agree to his plans without some token resistance, even though Spain was one of her favourite destinations and she was increasingly intrigued to meet the woman who had given Lincoln up as a baby.

What had been her reasons? Her circumstances? What had made her feel she had no choice but to hand her baby over to others to rear?

'People will expect us to have a short honeymoon. And I'd prefer you to meet Nina as soon as possible. Her health is unreliable. Her doctors can't seem to agree on how long she's got.'

Elodie could only imagine how sad it must have been for him to have finally found his birth mother, only to face the prospect of losing her all over again. He obviously cared about her, otherwise why go to the trouble and inconvenience of marrying his ex-fiancée, the woman who had publicly humiliated him seven years ago?

Elodie wanted to make a good impression on Nina—not for Lincoln's sake but for the woman herself. But how could she, given the train wreck of their history? How much had he told his birth mother about her? And what if Nina had already done her own research? The internet was full of the scandals that clung to her name, with the latest one naming her as the 'other woman' in a misnamed 'love triangle' that had seen a society wedding cancelled—eerily, like hers had been—at the altar.

Her twin, Elspeth, had been there, in a twin-switch, because Elodie had had a financial meeting that meant she hadn't been able to get there for the rehearsal in time. Then the meeting had been extended, which had given her the perfect excuse not to go to the wedding at all. She had dreaded the fallout if the bride had ever found out she'd had a one-night stand with the groom...

The only good to come out of it had been Elspeth meeting the groom's older brother, Mack MacDiarmid, and now they were happily in love and getting married in a month's time.

'But what if Nina doesn't like me?'

'She'll love you, because she believes you to be the love of my life.'

Elodie couldn't hold back another frown. 'Is that what you told her?'

His expression was unreadable. 'It's what she wants to believe.' He lifted his glass to his lips and drained the contents. He lowered the glass to the coffee table with a definitive thud and added, 'And you will do everything in your power to make sure she continues to believe it. Understood?'

Elodie gave him a mocking salute. 'Loud and clear.'

Lincoln held her defiant gaze for a beat or two. 'I'll pick you up at ten in the morning. Pack what you need for the time being, and anything else can be picked up later. I'll cover the rent on your flat for six months. The ceremony isn't until twelve, but we have some legal paperwork to see to first. And I'd appreciate it if you'd keep up appearances with all your friends and family and associates. We'll have a dinner celebration here with my family—and yours, if they can make it. I know it's short notice, but I don't want anyone to suspect our relationship isn't the real deal in case it gets back to Nina.'

'You mean lie to them?'

'I'm sure it won't impinge on your conscience too badly.' He flicked an invisible piece of lint off his rolled-up sleeve and continued, 'I heard about your deception at Fraser MacDiarmid's wedding. It created quite a scandal. How did Elspeth cope with pretending to be you for the weekend?'

'She got herself engaged to Mack MacDiarmid, so I'd say very well indeed. But that raises another issue. Their wedding's in a month's time, and since you and I'll be married you'll be expected to be there with me. It's likely to be a big affair. Will you be able to act like a devoted husband who's madly in love with his wife?'

'I'll do my best.'

'And we'll have to share a room if everyone thinks we're in love and sleeping together.'

The thought of it sent a tremor of unease through her body. Not because she was worried he would take advantage of such a situation, but because she wasn't sure she could resist him if he did. There was a particular intimacy about sharing a room, even if not sharing a bed. Taking turns to use the bathroom, dressing and undressing and moving about the space they shared… It would stir a host of memories she had spent the last seven years doing her level best to forget.

Lincoln's smile didn't reach his eyes. 'We will have to give the appearance of being in an intimate relationship at all times and in all places. And, judging from your kiss a few minutes ago, that's not going to be too hard for you to achieve.'

'That kiss was hardly one-sided. I thought you were going to make—'

'I wasn't.' His tone was adamant and it cut her like a knife. 'I meant what I said about the rules. A paper marriage is a lot easier to dissolve than a consummated one. Once the six months is up we'll get a simple annulment and move on with our lives.'

He made it sound so simple, so clinical, when her feelings about him and their arrangement were anything but. Six months as his wife on paper. Six months acting the role of devoted intimate partner. But another way of looking at it was to think of it as six months building her career, making the most of the time to launch her own label. Being Lincoln's wife would lift her profile like nothing else could.

His wife… How those words made her insides tighten with unruly desire.

Elodie leaned down to pick up her purse. 'I'd better get going. I'll need my beauty sleep for the big day tomorrow.'

Lincoln placed a hand on her wrist as she straightened. 'I won't be made a fool of twice.'

She held his determined gaze, her skin tingling where his fingers curled around the slender bones of her wrist. 'Nor will I.' She brushed off his hand with a stiff smile. 'Let's leave the intimate touching for when there's an audience, shall we? Or have you already changed your mind?'

A devilish glint appeared in his eyes. 'If I do, you'll be the first to know.'

CHAPTER THREE

ELODIE TOOK OVER an hour to decide what to wear for her wedding day. *Her wedding day.* What a mockery those words were in the context in which she was becoming Lincoln Lancaster's wife.

Her wedding day seven years ago had involved a team of hair and make-up experts, a designer gown and a hand-embroidered veil that had had a train two metres long. Her bridesmaids, including her twin, Elspeth, had attended her, along with a cute flower girl and a cheeky little boy who had been ring bearer. The church, complete with an angelic-sounding choir, had been packed with guests and flowers.

A fairy tale setting without the happy ending.

She didn't like to think too deeply about her regrets over how she'd ended her relationship with Lincoln. She knew she had hurt her mother and her twin—especially Elspeth, who'd had received a lot of undeserved criticism when everyone had assumed she must have known something.

But even Elodie hadn't truly known what she was going to do until she'd done it. It had been an impulsive decision that, at the time, had felt like her only option. She suspected the only hurt she had inflicted on Lincoln was to his pride. He hadn't been in love with her, so it wasn't as if his heart had been shattered by her jilting him. But even so, she did feel a twinge of guilt that she had bolted without talking to him face to face.

And now she was facing another wedding day with Lincoln. But what had changed in seven years? He still didn't love her, and he was only marrying her to give his birth mother her dying wish to see him settled. Elodie couldn't help feeling compromised about lying to someone who had so little time left. What if his mother saw through their act? What if his mother was like his housekeeper and disliked her on sight?

The streak of rebelliousness in Elodie's nature had her reaching for a black dress for their wedding. But then she thought of Lincoln's mother and changed her mind, and chose a cream one instead. There would be photos of the event, and no doubt they would go online. She couldn't afford for anything to look amiss—especially when she hoped to use her marriage to Lincoln as a platform to build her own success.

She made sure her hair and make-up were perfect, and she put on pearl earrings and a pearl necklace that teamed nicely with the classic cut of her calf-length dress.

The doorbell sounded and Elodie took a deep calming breath and addressed herself in the mirror. 'You can do this.'

* * *

The door opened and Lincoln's breath stalled in his throat. Elodie didn't have to try too hard to look stunning at the best of times, but right now she could have stopped traffic. Air traffic. Her cream dress had a swirly skirt with a chiffon overlay that fell to her shapely calves, and the upper part of the outfit clung to her curves in all the right places. Places he had touched, kissed and caressed in the past and wanted desperately to do so again.

His continued desire for her was a problem, given the terms of their marriage. He wanted no complications, and sleeping with Elodie Campbell would be one hell of a complication. Not because it wouldn't be exciting, thrilling and deeply satisfying—because it would be all that and more. But sleeping with her in the past had made him fall in love with her, and he couldn't allow his feelings to be triggered again. Besides, he was only allowing six months for their marriage. His mother's doctors hadn't been precise on her expected lifespan, but they had all agreed it would be a matter of three or four months, tops.

'You look stunning,' he managed to say once he could get his voice to work.

'I dragged this old thing out of the back of the wardrobe,' Elodie said. 'I figured you wouldn't want me to wear my old wedding dress.'

Lincoln frowned. 'Do you still have it?'

A fleeting sheepish look came over her face. 'It was custom-made and cost a fortune.'

'You could have sold it.'

'Nah, too much trouble.' She turned to collect her purse and keys and her phone off the small hall table. 'I keep it as a reminder not to do stupid things.'

'Do you still have your engagement ring?'

She turned to look at him with a frown pulling at her brow. 'I took it back to your house. Didn't you find it?'

'When did you bring it?'

'I dropped it off after I left the church when I... left. No one was home, so I used my key and left that as well, with a note.'

Lincoln wasn't sure he should believe her. The ring had been ridiculously expensive, and would have fetched a decent sum if she had sold it. He hadn't specifically asked for it back. He hadn't been interested in any contact with her after that humiliating day. But it had niggled at him all these years that she hadn't done the decent thing and at least offered to return it. And if she had returned it, why hadn't his housekeeper mentioned it? Surely Morag would have found it in her spring-cleaning efforts the following day? Trusting Elodie was not something he was prepared to do.

He slipped his hand inside his jacket pocket and took out a ring box and handed it to her. 'Just as well I have a backup.'

Elodie took the ring box from him, her forehead still cast in a small frown. She prised open the lid and stared at the classic halo diamond ring he had chosen. It was far simpler than the one he had purchased for her seven years ago, but no less expensive.

Money wasn't an issue for him when he had a goal to achieve. And making Elodie his wife for six months was his primary goal.

'Aren't you going to try it on?'

'Sure.' Elodie took the ring out and handed him back the box. She slipped the ring over her finger and held her hand up to the light to inspect the quality of the diamond. 'It's lovely. But I'll definitely give it back to you in person once we end our marriage.'

Lincoln held her gaze for a beat. 'No. You can keep it as a souvenir—like the wedding dress.'

She gave him a defiant look. 'I'm not the sentimental type.'

He gave a crooked smile and leaned down to pick up the two large suitcases near the door. She had never been one to travel light. 'Come on. We have some paperwork to sign before we get married.'

'You mean a pre-nuptial agreement? That sort of thing?' Elodie said on her way with him to his car.

'We both have assets to protect. As I said before—it will make an annulment a lot less complicated.'

'You didn't get me to sign one seven years ago.' There was an accusatory note in her voice.

'I didn't have as many assets back then, and nor did we actually get married, so it's a moot point.'

'But what if we had got married and subsequently divorced? Weren't you taking a risk by not insisting on a pre-nup?'

Lincoln shrugged one shoulder and opened the passenger door for her. 'Maybe I trusted you back then.'

'But you don't now?'

A wounded look came into her blue eyes. He held her gaze for a pulsing moment. 'Trust has to be earned once it's been broken.'

'I was never unfaithful to you. And I did bring back your damn engagement ring.'

She got into the passenger seat and swished the skirt of her dress out of the way, her expression stormy.

Lincoln closed the door of the car and walked around to the driver's side. He slipped in beside her and pulled down his seatbelt, clipped it into place. He turned to look at her, but she had turned her head to look the other way.

'Elodie, look at me.'

'No.'

He reached out his hand and captured her small, neat chin, gently turned her to face him. He frowned at the shimmer of tears in her eyes. He blotted an escaping one with the pad of his thumb.

'Tears?'

He couldn't keep the surprise out of his voice. He had never seen her cry—not even when they'd had furious arguments with each other in the past. She'd always given as good as she got and never resorted to floods of tears.

Elodie batted his hand away, her expression churlish. 'I'm not crying. It's just a reaction to my new eyeshadow. I—I think I must be allergic to it or something.'

Lincoln brushed his bent knuckles across the

creamy curve of her cheek. He couldn't stop his gaze from drifting to the plump contours of her mouth.

'Hey...'

His voice came out low and deep and husky, and her shimmering eyes crept up to meet his. Something in his chest came loose, like a tight knot unravelling. He brushed the pad of his thumb over the cushion of her lower lip, back and forth, watching as her pupils dilated and her lips softly parted. He leaned closer and lowered his mouth to hers in a feather-light kiss. It was a mere brush of his lips across her soft ones, but it sent a shockwave of ferocious lust through his body.

He eased back to gaze into her eyes before he was tempted to take the kiss deeper. 'Let's see if we can get through the rest of today without fighting, hmm?'

She brushed at her eyes with an impatient flick of her hand. 'Good luck with that.'

Their meeting with his lawyer was held in a smart office a few blocks from where they were to be married. There were documents to read and papers to sign, but Elodie found it almost impossible to concentrate. Her lips were still tingling from Lincoln's brief kiss in the car, and her emotions were see-sawing.

She couldn't remember the last time she had shed tears. She didn't do emotional displays—she had taught herself not to—but for some reason Lincoln's lack of trust in her had stung far more bitterly than it should. So what if he didn't believe her about the stupid engagement ring? She knew the truth, even if he didn't believe it.

How could two people be so unsuited to marry? They were enemies, not lovers. There was so much residual angst between them and yet they were about to become man and wife. Lincoln had called a truce, but how long would that last?

A short time later they arrived at the register office. Lincoln had organised two employees from his office to act as witnesses.

The ceremony was conducted with brisk efficiency and zero sentimentality. Had that been Lincoln's plan? To make this ceremony as different as it could possibly be from their wedding day seven years ago? There were no flowers, no angelic-sounding choir, no bridesmaids, no flower girl and impish little ring bearer. Just two people she had never met before, witnessing what was supposed to be the happiest day of one's life.

'You may now kiss the bride.'

Elodie was jolted out of her reverie when Lincoln drew her closer. His hands framed her face and his mouth came down to hers in a kiss that totally ambushed her senses.

His kiss was gentle, and yet passionate, tender and yet determined, and she was swept away on a rushing tide of longing. She forgot where they were…was not conscious of anything but the exquisite sensation of his lips moving sensually on hers. Her lips remembered every contour of his mouth, every movement of his lips as they stirred her senses into rapture.

She opened her mouth under the delicious pressure of his, and while he didn't deepen the kiss, it was no less thrilling. In fact, it intensified the experience, heightening all her senses to every subtle movement and sensation. The soft press of his lips on hers, the intake of his breath, the audible gasp of hers, the tilt of his head as he changed position, the slight rasp of his masculine skin against her soft feminine skin, the splay of his fingers as he cradled her face in his hands.

It was a kiss that stirred sleeping feelings into wakefulness—feelings Elodie had thought would never come back to life. Feelings she didn't want to come back to life because they threatened to take over her life and her dreams and aspirations.

That could *not* happen.

It *would* not happen.

She would not *let* it happen.

The repeated clicking of a camera shutter was the cue Elodie needed to pull away. She kept her features in a mask of pretend happiness for the photographer, knowing that every photo would be crucially important to achieving her goal.

Lincoln put his arm around her waist and led her outside, where some paparazzi were waiting. 'This shouldn't take too long,' he said in an undertone. 'Leave the talking to me.'

Elodie glanced up at him with a frown. 'Why? I can speak for myself. I handle the media all the time. Besides, I want to make the most of the attention on us. It will put a spotlight on my new label like nothing else could.'

His lips tightened momentarily, as if he was going

to argue the point with her, but then he gave a sigh. 'Fine, but don't overplay it.'

One of the journalists pressed forward with a recording device. 'Congratulations to you both. Can you tell us how you got back together?'

Elodie beamed at the journalist and leaned her head lovingly on Lincoln's broad shoulder. 'We realised we'd never fallen out of love and decided to get married as soon as we could.'

'We're happy to be together again,' Lincoln said, his arm around her waist tightening. He led her down a series of steps to the footpath, with the group of journalists moving backwards in order to keep snapping pictures.

'Lincoln, congratulations on winning back your runaway bride. Does this mean we'll be hearing the patter of tiny feet any time soon?'

'We haven't made any plans in that regard,' Lincoln said with a cool smile. 'Now, if you'll excuse us, we're looking forward to some time alone to celebrate our marriage.'

Lincoln led Elodie to his car, half a block away, with the paparazzi following all the way, taking numerous shots of them together. Elodie kept her blissful bride face on, but inside she was ruminating on his comment about children.

Did he still want children some time in the future? Obviously not with her, as their marriage was not going to be long-term. But did he one day want to settle down and raise a family, similar to the one he was raised in?

Even though she didn't feel any particularly strong maternal urges, she couldn't help feeling a twinge of jealousy that another woman, one day in the future, would be the mother of Lincoln's children. But what place did her jealousy have in a six-month marriage agreement? None. She had signed the paperwork and she had accepted the terms. Their marriage was not the happy-ever-after type. It was an agreement so that she could receive the necessary finance for her label and Lincoln could assure his mother, before she died, that he was finally settled with the 'love of his life'.

Lincoln helped Elodie into his car and was soon behind the driver's seat and pulling away from the kerb. 'Nice work back there. You almost had me convinced you'd fallen madly in love with me.'

'Ha-ha.' Elodie gave him the side-eye and then turned to smile sweetly for the lingering journalists. Once they had driven clear of the paparazzi, she twisted in her seat to look at him. 'That comment you made about kids back there to the paps... *Are* you planning on having a family one day? I mean, after we end this arrangement?'

There was no change in his expression, but his fingers tightened ever so slightly on the steering wheel. 'No.'

Elodie frowned. 'But when we were together seven years ago you talked about having a family.'

'That was then—this is now.'

'I understand that you don't want any kids with me, especially since we'll only be married a matter of months, but I thought you'd still want to—'

'I don't.' His tone was curt.

'But why?'

His gaze was fixed on the road ahead, his jaw set as hard as granite. 'Meeting my biological mother changed my mind.'

'But I thought you liked her? She's obviously someone you care about, otherwise why would you be marrying me to make her happy in her final months of life?'

He sent her a grim look. 'I care deeply about her.'

'Have you met your biological father?'

'He died before I was born.' There was no trace of emotion in his voice, and yet she sensed a deep sadness behind his dispassionate answer.

'How?'

'Car crash.'

'How sad for your mother. Did that have something to do with why she gave you up?'

'We haven't discussed it much. She seems reluctant to talk about it, so I don't push it.'

Elodie studied his inscrutable features. What was the story behind his conception?

Thankfully, the forced adoptions of several generations ago were no longer common. Most women who relinquished a baby these days did so because they wanted their child to have better opportunities than they could provide. It was still a difficult decision, and no doubt there were still elements of pressure on some women from their family of origin. But these days there were safety measures in place to give the relinquishing mother a chance to change her mind during the process of adoption. There was even open adoption now, where children maintained their contact with the birth mother while being raised by adoptive parents.

'How are your brother and sister?' she asked.

'Aiden and Sylvia are both doing well.'

Elodie nibbled at her lower lip for a moment. 'Are they adopted as well?'

'No, my parents naturally conceived Aiden a year after adopting me, then Sylvia came eighteen months after him.'

'Wow, that's amazing. But did it make you feel on the outside at all?'

'Not really. My parents were devoted to us all, and my mother in particular insisted that she wouldn't have been able to have her own children if I hadn't come along. She said it so often I eventually believed it.'

'She sounds like she was an amazing person.'

'She was.'

Elodie had seen photos in the past of his family, and never once questioned Lincoln's place in it. She had even met them in person at their engagement party, and they had seemed like a normal family. He even looked a little like his adoptive father, Clive. It still hurt that he hadn't told her he was adopted. It made her feel shut out and insignificant—feelings which had added to the reasons she had run away from their wedding day.

'How did Aiden and Sylvia take the news of our reunion? Are they coming tonight to celebrate?'

'They're looking forward to seeing you again.'

She glanced at him in surprise. 'So they've forgiven me for jilting you?'

'You'll have to ask them yourself.'

She rolled her eyes and gushed out a theatrical sigh. '*Really* looking forward to that.'

He gave a wry sound of amusement. 'Did you manage to convince any of your family to come tonight?'

'Actually, Elspeth and Mack happen to be in London at the moment, so they'll come. Which reminds me—Elspeth has a serious nut allergy, remember? I'll have to talk to Morag about making sure her food is not contaminated.'

'I've already spoken to her.'

'Thanks, but I'm not afraid of her, you know.'

Elodie was touched he'd remembered her twin's allergy, but wouldn't have minded a showdown with Morag to establish some boundaries. *Start as you mean to go on*, was her credo now. She was not going to allow the housekeeper to walk all over her feelings this time around.

'I know, but I want things to go as smoothly as possible.'

Elodie shrugged and continued. 'Mum can't come, but not because she didn't want to—she's in Ireland with her new partner, visiting his family.'

She decided against telling him she had told her twin the truth about their marriage. She could trust Elspeth to keep quiet and play along with the charade.

'Were your mother and Elspeth surprised by your announcement?'

'Mum is impossible to surprise these days. I think it's because of all the impulsive things I've done in the past.'

He gave a wry *been-there-experienced-that-first-hand* grunt. 'What about Elspeth? Was she surprised when you told her?'

She swivelled in her seat to look at him. 'No, because she thinks you've always been in love with me.'

Lincoln's mouth tightened just a fraction. 'Then let's hope she keeps that fantasy going for the next six months.' He changed gear and added, 'Is your father coming tonight?'

Elodie gave a mirthless laugh. 'No way. I know better than to ask him. He's always got something more important to do.'

She felt rather than saw the weight of Lincoln's glance on her, and mentally kicked herself for revealing her father issues. Showing vulnerability was a no-no in a relationship such as theirs. A transactional relationship that had no place for sharing emotional baggage. Not that she had ever shared much of her baggage in the past... She hated showing any sign of emotional neediness, especially to someone like Lincoln, who was so in control of his emotions—if he had any, that was.

'What about your father? Has he forgiven me too?'

'You won't have any problems on that score. He forgave you long ago.'

But have you? Elodie wanted to ask, but she stayed silent.

If the roles had been reversed, she would have

found it near impossible to forgive him if he had jilted her. Rejection was her worst nightmare.

Her fear of being abandoned came from her childhood. Her father had proudly paraded his cute twin girls around until they'd stopped being cute. As a young child Elodie had gravitated towards her father, because her mother had been so obsessed with keeping Elspeth safe from her nut allergy.

Elodie had thought she was her father's favourite, like Elspeth was her mother's. But how wrong she had been. She'd lost her first tooth and her father in the same week. He'd moved on to build a new life and a family with another woman. He hadn't even made the time to come to her ill-fated wedding.

But then, why would he have needed to? He had given her away years ago.

CHAPTER FOUR

THE CELEBRATORY DINNER was not something Lincoln was particularly looking forward to, but he was immensely glad of the distraction. Acting the devoted husband was going to be a stretch, but he preferred it to the alternative. Going home to be alone with Elodie until they flew to Spain the following day was too tempting to think about.

Their kiss at the wedding ceremony had stirred up a host of erotic memories he had tried for years to suppress. The hands-off paper marriage he was insisting on was not going to last long if he didn't pull himself into line. He needed to prove to himself that he could resist her this time around. But resisting her would be so much easier if he could ignore the way she lit up a room as soon as she entered it.

It wasn't just her natural beauty—it was her vibrant energy that spoke to him on a cellular level. He had never met a more exciting lover, and the thought of revisiting their passion was a persistent background hum in his body. A hum he was finding it increasingly difficult to ignore.

Lincoln led the way inside his house and then shrugged off his jacket and hung it over one of the velvet wing chairs in the foyer. 'We have a couple of hours before our guests arrive. I have some emails to deal with in my office. I'll leave you to re-familiarise yourself with the house. Morag has put you in the guest room next to mine.'

Elodie raised her neat eyebrows, her eyes alight with mischief. 'The one with the connecting door?'

Lincoln flattened his mouth into a firm line. 'The door will remain locked.'

She raised her chin, her eyes still glinting. 'Which side is the key on?'

He had to force himself not to stare at the perfect curve of her mouth. That pillow-soft mouth he could still taste on his lips. 'My side.'

She made a moue with her lips. 'Shouldn't there be one on my side too? I mean, fair's fair and all that.'

'I can't imagine any circumstances in which you would need to enter my room.'

Elodie's eyes danced as they held his in a challenging look. 'Oh, can't you?'

A hot shiver ran down his spine and set spot fires in his groin. He reached up to his neck to loosen his tie, which right then was all but strangling him. 'I'll see you later.'

He began to walk away, but one of her slim hands landed on his forearm in a light but electrifying hold. Another shiver shimmied down his spine and hot, hard heat filled his pelvis.

'Don't you think we should rehearse how we're going to behave in front of our guests tonight?'

'Rehearse?'

She moved closer, sliding her hand down his arm, her fingers ever so lightly brushing over the back of his hand. His skin tingled and his pulse quickened. He could smell the exotic notes of her signature scent—a mix of musk, tuberose and something that was unique to her.

'We'll need to look comfortable touching each other like lovers do.'

Her smile had a sultry tilt that made the heat in his groin smoulder to boiling point.

'Right now, you look tense and uncomfortable.'

Tense was right. He had never felt so hard in his life. He placed his hands on her wrists, intending to put her away from him, but somehow, he found himself doing the opposite. The magnetic pull of her body called out to the humming need in his. He brought her flush against him, not caring that she could feel every throbbing beat of his blood against her lower body.

'Is this the sort of thing you mean? Getting up close and personal?' He kept his tone cynical, but his mind was whirling with the possibility of tweaking the rules.

Elodie moved against him, her yielding softness against his hardness sending a torrent of lust through him. She eased her wrists out of his hold and wound her arms around his neck, her cinnamon-scented breath teasing his senses into overdrive.

'You want me so bad…'

Her voice had a throaty quality to it that only did more lethal damage to his self-control. Lincoln put his hands on her slim hips, holding her to the jutting ridge of his arousal. The feel of her against him sent his senses spinning. She was impossible to resist in this playfully seductive mood. But resist he must.

'We'll embarrass our guests if we don't show some restraint.' His gaze lowered to her mouth and his heart rate spiked. 'Kissing is fine, holding hands, hugging…but that's all.'

Elodie stepped on tiptoe and planted a soft-as-air kiss to his lips. She pulled away so slowly her lips clung to his like silk catching on something rough.

She sent the tip of her tongue over her lips and smiled at him, her eyes still twinkling. 'Is that chaste enough for you, baby?'

Her purring tone was almost his undoing. *Almost.* He knew she was toying with him and he wasn't going to be so easily manipulated—even though every male hormone in his body was begging him to give in to the temptation she was dangling before him. No one could turn him on like Elodie Campbell. Smart, sassy, sophisticated, sexy—all the things her brand defined her as were catnip to him. But he had to resist her for as long as he could. To prove to himself she no longer had the power over him she'd once had.

Lincoln took her by the upper arms and put her from him, keeping his expression impassive. 'You're playing a dangerous game, sweetheart. And you won't win it.'

Elodie gave a carefree laugh and reached up and

pulled her long hair out of its updo, letting the silken tresses fall about her shoulders in fragrant bouncing waves. 'Don't bet on it.'

She blew him a kiss and turned on her sky-high heels and walked away, leaving him burning, burning, burning with rabid lust.

Elodie entered the bedroom next to Lincoln's and closed the door and leaned back against it with a whooshing sigh. She knew it was dangerous, tempting Lincoln into changing his mind about the terms of their marriage. But knowing he wanted her gave her a sense of power—an addictive sense of power she couldn't resist exercising.

Lincoln was a man who held strong opinions. Once he made up his mind he found it difficult to change it. It was one of the reasons they'd locked horns so much in the past. They were both strong-willed and opinionated and neither of them wanted to back down.

If by some miracle she managed to change his mind, she would be flirting with even more danger. The danger of allowing her feelings into the passion they shared. That had been her mistake in the past— falling for him because he was such a fabulous lover. She had confused physical chemistry with emotional attachment. How had she been so foolish to not recognise it? Just because a man knew how to make your blood sing, it didn't mean he was in love with you.

Seven years ago, Lincoln might have been in lust with her—just as he was now—but love had never been part of his commitment to her. He had been willing to marry her, to live with her and have a family with her, but he hadn't been willing to offer her his heart. What sort of star-struck, lovesick idiot had she been to accept him on those terms back then?

Since their breakup Elodie had never felt anything for any of her lovers—not that there had been many. She had actively encouraged a party girl image to go with her smart, successful, sassy, sophisticated and sexy brand. Those five *S*-words sold the lingerie and swimwear she modelled. But no one had come close to exciting her the way Lincoln had.

Sex for her had been a purely mechanical thing before she'd met him. She had never orgasmed with a lover before him and she hadn't since. It was as if he had cursed her to be unable to fully function sexually without him. Which was part of her reason for wanting to revisit their passion. She needed to know if he still had the same sensual power over her. Judging from the kisses they had shared, it was looking highly likely.

Why was he so insistent on keeping their marriage on paper? It didn't make sense. They both stood to gain from their arrangement—why not exploit it to the fullest extent?

Elodie came downstairs a few minutes before their guests were due to arrive. She wandered into the kitchen to get a glass of water and came face to face with Morag, the housekeeper. A shiver of apprehension scuttled over her flesh, her heart-rate increased and a sense of dread as heavy as stone filled her stomach. She mentally prepared herself for attack, knowing it would be a miracle for the housekeeper to welcome her with open arms, especially after the way she had left Lincoln standing at the altar seven years ago.

She hid her unease behind a breezy smile. 'Hi, Morag. Nice to see you again.'

The older woman's lips pursed. 'So, you're back.'

Elodie waved a hand in front of her body. 'As you see. And blissfully happy. Aren't you going to congratulate me?'

'Congratulations.'

Never had someone sounded less sincere.

'Thanks. It's nice to be back.'

Morag wiped her hands on a tea towel and tossed it to one side, her expression set in disapproving lines. 'How long are you staying this time?'

Elodie gave a tinkling laugh. 'For ever, of course.'

The lie slipped off her tongue with such ease it was almost scary.

Morag harrumphed and picked up a paring knife. She began slicing into an avocado, her brow heavily furrowed. 'If I thought you truly loved him I'd be happy for you.'

Her voice had the stern quality of a buttoned-up schoolmistress dealing with a rebellious child.

Elodie shrugged off the housekeeper's comment with a nonchalant up-and-down movement of one shoulder. 'You're entitled to your opinion, I guess.'

Morag glanced at her with a narrow-eyed look. 'He deserves better than the likes of you.'

Elodie tried to suppress the bubble of anger that

rose in her chest, but it was like trying to hold back a flood. And along with the toxic tide of anger there was a deep twinge of hurt because the housekeeper saw her as a taker, not a giver.

She wasn't by nature a people-pleaser. She went her own way and didn't give a damn what people thought about her—or at least she pretended she didn't give a damn. What was it about her that Lincoln's housekeeper disliked so much? It had irritated her in the past, but now, for some strange reason, it hurt as well. Was there something about her that both Morag and her father saw? A flaw that made her unacceptable? Unlikeable? Unlovable?

She moved to the other side of the kitchen to find a glass, but because the kitchen had been remodelled she couldn't find one. 'Where do you keep the glasses?'

'Third cupboard on the right.'

'Thank you.' Elodie found a glass and took it over to the sink and filled it with water. She drank the water and then placed the glass upside down on the draining board. Then she turned and leaned back against the sink to look at the housekeeper. 'Did you know Lincoln was adopted when we were together seven years ago?'

Morag continued artfully arranging the sliced avocado on the seafood starters she was making for dinner. 'I knew.'

Elodie couldn't hold back a frown. He'd told his housekeeper and not her? How was that supposed to make her feel? How could she not feel upset and unimportant? Someone under his employ knew the intimate details of his life, and yet the woman he had asked to marry him did not. He had chosen *not* to tell her.

'Did he ask you not to mention it to me?'

Morag lifted her gaze from her food preparation to meet hers. 'I only knew because his mother Rosemary mentioned it to me in passing one day. Lincoln never told me himself and I didn't see it as my business to tell anyone else.'

'Not even his fiancée? The woman he'd chosen to be his wife?'

The housekeeper gave her an unwavering look. 'I think you already know the answer to that question. It's why you didn't go ahead with the wedding. You didn't love him the way he deserves to be loved.'

Elodie pushed herself away from the sink in agitation. Her feelings about Lincoln had always been the issue. The depth, the intensity, the overwhelming need of him she knew could put her in a vulnerable situation from which she might never escape.

'I wasn't ready for marriage back then. I was young—only twenty-one.'

'And you're ready now?' Scepticism was ripe in the housekeeper's tone.

Elodie straightened her shoulders, her chin at a defiant height. 'You bet I am.'

The first guests to arrive were Elspeth and Mack. Seeing her twin hand in hand with her gorgeous Scottish fiancé made Elodie feel faintly jealous. Not that she wasn't happy for her twin—she was. It was so nice to see her shy and reserved sister enjoying all the things she had missed out on before. But it was obvious Mack adored Elspeth—he could barely take his eyes off her and Elspeth glowed like never before. She was practically incandescent with love.

Elodie had once fooled herself that Lincoln looked at her the same way Mack did her twin. But she had mistaken lust for love and she wasn't going to be so stupid as to do so again. But the lust was real. It still throbbed between them and she was determined to bring him to his knees with it.

She smiled a secret smile. She knew how to seduce Lincoln. She had done it so many times before. He was holding out on her to prove a point. He wanted control this time around. But so did she. And she would damn well get it.

While Lincoln was chatting to Mack, Elodie quickly lured her twin aside to speak to her in private. She led Elspeth to a small room a few doors down from the formal dining room and closed the door once they were inside. 'Els, you're not supposed to know my marriage to Lincoln isn't the real deal, so please keep it under wraps. And, whatever you do, don't tell Mum.'

Elspeth frowned. 'But what about Mack? I've already told him and—'

Elodie let out a stiff curse. 'Will he say something to Lincoln, do you think?'

'I don't think so. He's the soul of discretion at the best of times.'

'Better have a word to him, just to make sure.'

Elspeth took one of Elodie's hands in hers. 'You probably should tell Lincoln that I know. It's not good to keep secrets in a marriage.'

Elodie gave a cynical cough of a laugh. 'Try telling Lincoln that. He's the one who didn't tell me anything about himself when we were together before.'

'Maybe you didn't spend enough time getting to know him. You did have rather a whirlwind relationship.'

'Look who's talking!'

Elspeth blushed a delightful shade of pink, her blue eyes shining with happiness. 'I know, right? It was crazily fast, and I still can't believe Mack and I are getting married next month. He's everything I ever dreamed of in a partner. I only wish you and Lincoln could sort things out and be—'

'Not much chance of that,' Elodie said, and opened the door to return to the dining room. 'Come on. Mean Morag, the crotchety old dragon of a housekeeper, will blame me if dinner is spoilt.'

Lincoln watched Elodie and her twin walk together into the dining room, where the other guests were assembled. The twins were eerily alike, but while he had only seen them together a handful of times, he could always tell them apart. Elspeth was a more introverted and reserved version of Elodie. But that was what had drawn him to Elodie in the first place—her vibrant zest for life and her devil-may-care attitude. She didn't just dare to step where angels feared to tread—she stomped in with her sky-high heels and laughed while she did it.

She was smiling now, her beautiful white teeth framed by a vivid red lipstick, her make-up perfect, her hair a voluminous cloud around her slim shoulders. She had changed into a tight-fighting black dress that clung to her feminine curves in a way that made him fantasise about peeling it off her later.

But the rules were the rules and he needed them in place. He had rushed into a fling with her in the past and it had blown up in his face. This time he wanted control. And falling madly in love and lust all over again was not going to help him maintain it.

Elodie came over to him and nestled against his side, gazing up at him adoringly. He had never said she wasn't a good actor. No one would ever think she wasn't thrilled about being married to him. But then, she was getting a heap of publicity out of their reunion. The photos of their wedding had already gone viral, and he was fielding dozens of requests for an exclusive interview. No doubt so was she.

Lincoln slipped his arm around her waist, the feel of her against his side sending shivers down his spine. 'Come and say hello to Dad, and to Aiden and Sylvia and their partners.'

He led her to where his family were gathered, enjoying the drinks and nibbles provided by Morag.

'Welcome home, Elodie, my dear,' Clive Lancaster said with a warm smile. 'This is my partner, Jan.'

Elodie smiled and greeted everyone in turn. 'It's

so nice to see you all again. And so good of you to be here to celebrate with us tonight at such short notice.'

Clive clapped a hand on Lincoln's shoulder, his eyes shining with warmth and fatherly affection. 'I wouldn't have missed it for anything. I've waited a long time for Lincoln to settle down with the only woman he has ever loved. And maybe I'll get those grandbabies now, eh?'

'Ri-i-i-ght...' Lincoln smiled and ignored the twinge of guilt in his gut about the truth of his marriage to Elodie.

He didn't like lying to his family, but needs must in this case. He had to provide his biological mother with the peace she longed for before she passed away. Nina still agonised over her decision to relinquish him as a baby. She longed to see him happily settled, to have the assurance that her decision hadn't permanently damaged his ability to love and be loved.

But love wasn't part of his arrangement with Elodie and nor had it ever been, in spite of her regular and gushing declarations of it in the past. If she'd loved him she wouldn't have jilted him. In his mind it was a simple as that. If she had truly had deep feelings for him she would have expressed her concerns about their relationship—not left him standing in front of a congregation of guests looking like a fool.

There was a part of him that would never forgive her for that. The humiliation had stung then and it still stung now—which was why he was keeping firm control of the way things would play out between them going forward.

* * *

Elodie sipped glass after glass of champagne and nibbled at the delicious food the housekeeper had placed in front of her and the other guests. Lincoln was seated at the head of the long dining table, his father at the other end. Elodie was on his left and felt acutely conscious of everyone—particularly the members of his family, who were watching her every movement, gesture or expression.

Her face was aching from smiling, and her brain was fried from trying to make convivial conversation with everyone. Normally she loved a good party. She could work any room like a pro without a moment's worry about putting a foot wrong or, indeed, about what anyone thought of her.

But for some reason it felt wrong to be pretending to Lincoln's family that their relationship was genuine. The only thing that was genuine was the lust simmering between them. She was aware of the pulse of it every time Lincoln took her hand, his fingers warm and strong around hers. Every time he locked gazes with her, every time he brought her hand up to his mouth and kissed her bent knuckles, or the ends of her fingers, a lightning-fast current of erotic energy passed from his body to hers, leaving her wanting, wanting, wanting…

Clive rose towards the end of the meal, glass in hand. 'Let's toast the happy couple. To Lincoln and Elodie. May your future be bright and happy and fulfilling and blessed with children.'

Elodie reached for her glass but, anxious, somehow managed to knock it over instead. 'Oops.'

Lincoln righted the glass and refilled it within seconds. He held his glass against hers. 'To us.'

She clinked her glass against his, her expression as radiant as her twin's. 'To us.'

But then, she was good at masking her true feelings. No one would ever guess at the turmoil inside her at the thought of having Lincoln's baby. He didn't love her. How could she raise a family with someone who didn't love her? It was asking for heartbreak. The sort of heartbreak she had run away from seven years ago. The sort of heartbreak her mother had suffered.

Where was the 'for ever love' Elodie's father had once claimed to feel for his wife and his cute twin daughters? It had gone away like a wisp of smoke as soon as someone more interesting came along.

'Now for the first dance,' said Sylvia, Lincoln's young sister. 'Go on, you two. Show us your moves.'

Elodie wasn't the type of person to blush, but as soon as Lincoln gathered her in his arms a rush of heat flowed from her cheeks to her core. He held her close, hip to hip, thigh to thigh, cheek to cheek, as they danced to the music Aiden had jumped up to put on the sophisticated sound system.

It was a romantic ballad that was poignant and bittersweet—which perfectly described her situation. It wouldn't matter if she were married to Lincoln for six months or six decades. She would never be able to guarantee he would love her the way she longed to be loved. He could *act* as if he did. No one looking at him now would think he wasn't madly in love with her. But she was too much of cynic to think he would ever open his heart to her. She was still a trophy wife—a beautiful bit of arm candy to show off to his dying mother and convince her she hadn't done the wrong thing in relinquishing him as a baby.

Lincoln tipped up her chin and looked into her eyes. 'Did I tell you how beautiful you look tonight?'

Elodie smiled, even though his words kind of proved her point. He loved the way she *looked*. He didn't love *her*.

'You look pretty damn awesome yourself.' She linked her arms around his neck and swayed against him with the music. 'You feel pretty damn awesome too.'

His hands grasped her hips but he didn't separate their bodies. He brought her harder against him, in spite of their watchful audience. His blue-green gaze blazed with lust…the same lust she could feel pounding in her own body.

He lowered his mouth to just below her ear, his lips sending shivers coursing down her spine as he spoke in an undertone. 'You're enjoying yourself a little too much, aren't you?'

Elodie gave a breathy laugh and rolled her head further to one side, to give him better access to the sensitive skin of her neck. 'You're making it hard not to enjoy myself. No one would ever think you weren't desperate to get me alone right now.'

His hands tightened on her hips and his lips moved

across her skin as lightly as a feather, stirring her nerves into a frenzy.

'I am desperate to get you alone…but not for the reason you think.'

His voice was a low, rough burr of sound that made her spine tingle from top to bottom. She framed his face in her hands, staring into his eyes with brazen defiance. 'You mean you're *not* going to make mad, passionate love to me on our wedding night?'

'You know the rules.'

His eyes glinted with determination and she could feel the war going on in his body. He was fighting their mutual attraction, but she was confident she would bring him down.

She smiled a sultry smile. 'I just love it when you draw a line in the sand.'

'Why?'

'Because I get such a kick out of stepping over it.'

And then she planted her lips on his.

CHAPTER FIVE

FOR A MOMENT Lincoln forgot they weren't alone. As soon as her lips met his a fire erupted in his body. An inferno of lust that left no part of him unaffected. His groin tightened, the backs of his legs tingled and his self-control scrambled to get back on duty.

But it was always this way with Elodie. Her passionate and rebellious nature spoke to him in a raw, primal way that was nothing short of overwhelming. Need pummelled through his flesh, making him hot and tight within seconds.

He had existed for seven years without this heady rush of excitement. How had he done it? It seemed impossible that he had lived in a wasteland of substandard sensuality when he could have had this fiery intensity of lust. Her mouth was soft and yet insistent, and he answered it with the thrust of his tongue, mating with hers in a playful duel that sent another rush of blood to his groin.

'Get a honeymoon suite, you guys!' called out his brother Aiden with a laugh.

Lincoln lifted his mouth off Elodie's with a cynical smile only she could see. 'We'll finish this later.'

One way or the other, he *had* to get control of his desire for her. She was exploiting it and he was in danger of caving in like a horny teenager lusting over his first crush.

'Ooh, I can hardly wait.' Her eyes danced with mischief and she eased out of his arms to go and sit next to her twin.

Lincoln went back to the table and pretended to listen to a conversation between Mack and his father. He picked up his wine glass and took a token sip, but no amount of alcohol could make him as drunk as Elodie's sexy mouth. That soft and supple mouth had in the past been all over his body, sending him to the stratosphere multiple times.

He suppressed a shudder and picked up his water glass instead and took a long draught. He put the glass back on the table and caught Elodie's eye. She smiled and gave him a fingertip wave, and another rush of heat flowed through his flesh.

It was probably only a few minutes later that everyone began to leave, but to Lincoln it was like hours. Finally, the door closed on the last of their guests and Lincoln and Elodie returned to the dining room, where Morag was busy clearing everything away.

'Let me help you with that,' Elodie said, stepping forward to help stack some plates.

'Leave it,' Morag said, without even turning from the table to look at Elodie. 'You'll only end up breaking something.'

Lincoln frowned at his housekeeper's clipped tone. He had never heard her be so brusque with Elodie— or indeed with anyone before. But then, Morag hadn't seen him enter the room with Elodie, as her back was to the door. He'd always thought Elodie had exaggerated the housekeeper's behaviour towards her in the past. Elodie was a bit of a drama queen and liked being the centre of attention. Morag's no-nonsense, stay-in-the-background personality was the total opposite. But now he wondered if he would have done better to keep an open mind. He had known his housekeeper a lot longer than Elodie and sided with her. Had that been a mistake?

Elodie continued stacking the plates, her lips in a tight line, her handling of the top-shelf crockery not exactly gentle. The clatter and clang of cutlery and china was obviously her way of showing how upset she was.

'It may surprise you, Morag, but I'm quite domesticated these days. I can stack a dishwasher, do my own laundry and cook a decent meal.'

'You'll need more skills than that to keep your husband happy,' Morag shot back.

Elodie placed the plates on the trolley that would ferry them back to the kitchen. 'I have plenty of *those* skills too.'

Her tone was pure sass, and her *don't-mess-with-me* expression a warning even he took note of. He knew all about those skills of hers. The sensual skills that gave him thrills like no other person ever had before or since. The sensual skills he was trying not to be tempted by. But he realised he had vastly under-estimated the explosive chemistry that still existed between them. Would it lessen if he indulged it or would it get out of control?

'Morag, why don't you leave this for us to clear away?' Lincoln said. 'You've worked long enough today. Go home and we'll see you when we get back from Spain.'

Morag turned from the table and wiped her hands on her apron, her expression unrepentant. 'She'll only bring you trouble. She doesn't love you.'

'It's none of your damn business *what* I feel about him,' Elodie flashed back, blue eyes blazing.

'Elodie—' Lincoln began in a calming tone, but she was having none of it.

'You always side with her,' Elodie said, turning to him. 'I'm your *wife*, for God's sake. You're supposed to… Oh, never mind.' She tossed the cutlery she was holding with a loud clatter on top of the plates on the trolley. 'I'm going to bed.'

She stalked out, slamming the door behind her.

Lincoln sighed and raked a hand through his hair. Drama and Elodie were never far away from each other, but he would have to get used to it—and so would his housekeeper. Otherwise the following six months would be unbearable.

Sacking Morag wasn't an option. She had been a stalwart support for more years than he could count—first to his mother, as a long-term friend, and since his mother's death Morag had been his link to her—one he wasn't ready to sever. She often gave him little vignettes of the two of them growing up as close friends, stories of their escapades and adventures and childhood games that kept his mother alive for him in his mind.

'Morag, go easy on her, yeah? I want things to work this time.'

The housekeeper's mouth tightened. 'She'll break your heart again. You mark my words.'

He wanted to tell his housekeeper that he hadn't had his heart broken, just his pride, but Morag had witnessed first-hand the fallout from Elodie jilting him.

'I'm not going to allow anything like that to happen,' he said, with the utmost confidence.

He was in control now. Emotions were not part of their relationship this time around and he was going to keep it that way.

Elodie was in her en suite bathroom, taking off her make-up, when there was a knock at the door. 'Go away.'

'Come on, sweetheart, open up,' Lincoln said, rapping his knuckles on the door again.

She slammed the toner bottle down on the counter and tossed the cotton pad in the bin. She opened the door and glared at him. 'If you've come to give me a lecture about being nicer to your housekeeper, then you're wasting my time and yours.'

'I've come to apologise.'

Elodie knew she shouldn't be mollified so easily, but something about his tone made her anger melt away. Her shoulders went down on a sigh and she came out of the bathroom, tightening the ties of her wrap around her waist a little more firmly.

'You're seven years too late with your apology.' She threw him a petulant look from beneath her lowered lashes. 'She's always been unnecessarily rude to me.'

Lincoln came over to her and raised her chin with his index finger, locking his gaze on hers. 'I'm sorry I didn't listen to you about that in the past. I can see there's tension between you.'

Elodie made a scoffing noise. 'Tension? You don't know the half of it.'

He placed his hands on her shoulders and gave them a gentle squeeze. 'I thought you didn't care what people thought of you?'

She lowered her gaze from his to stare at the collar of his shirt. 'I don't. But I don't think someone you employ to take care of your house should treat your… your…wife like she's gold-digging trailer trash. I earn my own money—heaps of it, actually. Not enough to launch my own label, but still…'

Lincoln raised her chin again, to mesh his gaze with hers. 'I've spoken to Morag and you shouldn't have any trouble in future.'

'And if I do?'

He drew in a breath and released it in a long exhalation. 'Then I'll deal with it.'

'How? By firing her?'

He released her, stepped back and rubbed a hand over his face. 'I don't know. She's worked for me a long time. She was a friend of my mother's—they went to primary school together. She had a rough time growing up, then she married a brute of a man who physically abused her every chance he got. They had a couple of kids who both ran off the rails and barely speak to her now. She finally got the courage to leave him and has worked for me ever since. Plus, she developed Type Two diabetes recently. She would probably find it hard to get another job that pays as well and with such flexible hours.'

Elodie sat on the edge of the bed with her hands resting either side of her thighs. She was secretly impressed by his commitment to his housekeeper. Morag was clearly a vulnerable person who had been taken advantage of in the past. Her heart ached for her and what she had been through. It was no wonder she didn't find it easy to let people into her life. It reminded her a little bit of herself.

'My God. I'm sorry to hear Morag has been through all that. She doesn't deserve to be treated that way. No one does. But hurt people don't heal themselves by hurting others. You have to work through your own pain rather than project it on to someone else.'

Lincoln twisted his mouth into a grimace. 'I guess that's how it plays out sometimes. She's a little set in her ways.'

Elodie flopped backwards on the bed, flinging her arms above her head. 'Oh, God, I'm so tired of how the world can hurt people. It's one of the reasons I want to work for myself. You would not believe the rubbish I've had to put up with for years.'

Lincoln came and sat beside her on the bed, but he didn't touch her. Even knowing he was within touching distance made every cell in her body throb with awareness.

'What sort of stuff? Sexual harassment?' His frown was heavy, his expression gravely serious.

She rolled her eyes like marbles in a jar. 'Nothing I couldn't handle on my own.'

He reached out and brushed a strand of hair back from her forehead. 'You shouldn't have to handle that stuff on your own. That stuff shouldn't happen in the first place.'

'Yeah, well, it still does.' She rolled over so she was facing him on her side, even more conscious of how close his body was to hers. 'Thanks for listening. I don't talk to anyone about this stuff except Elspeth, and half the time I don't tell her the full extent of it. It would shock her too much.'

'You try to be strong for her, don't you?'

Elodie let out a puff of air. 'Yes, well... I'm not the one with the life-threatening allergy, am I? When our father left...' She frowned and then continued, 'I didn't see it coming, you know? I thought he would always be there for us, and for me in particular, because he always called me his favourite girl. It was all lies. He didn't love anyone but himself.'

'I'm sorry you had such a jerk of a father. I can only imagine how that has impacted on you.'

Elodie met Lincoln's gaze, finding in it a warmth

and an emotional connection that was completely disarming. 'I think I've spent a lot of my life pretending to be someone I'm not. The cutesy outgoing twin, the cheeky extroverted kid who caused drama wherever she went. The blissfully happy bride-to-be...until I got cold feet, when the reality of being your wife—anyone's wife, for that matter—hit me.' She twisted her mouth and continued, 'I've had to be tough all my life. And I can see now why Morag is the way she is. It's emotional armour to keep from getting hurt.'

His eyes held hers, his pupils dark as black holes in outer space. 'It was never my intention to hurt you or block you from your dreams.' He took one of her hands in his and gave it a gentle squeeze. 'I wish you'd talked to me about this stuff way back then.'

'Yes, well... We didn't do a lot of talking, as I remember. Apart from arguing. And then having make-up sex.' She gave a rueful smile and continued, 'It was nice being with your family tonight, although I couldn't help feeling guilty about all the pretence.' She frowned and added, 'I can't help worrying that they'll be terribly hurt when we end this. I mean, your father seemed so convinced I'm the love of your life.' She gave an incredulous laugh and added, 'I can't imagine being the love of *anyone*'s life. I'm too much hard work.'

Lincoln stroked his fingers through her hair in a slow, mesmerising fashion, sending shivers over her scalp and down her spine.

'Sometimes hard work brings its own rewards.'

His eyes became hooded and drifted to her mouth,

and a wave of longing coursed through her. He leaned on one elbow, his other hand stroking up and down the length of her satin-covered thigh.

'I like your sister's fiancé, Mack. They seem a good match.'

'Yes, she's very happy and I'm happy for her.' Elodie toyed with one of the buttons on his shirt and added, 'I consider myself a bit of a matchmaker, actually. If I hadn't got her to go in my place to the wedding she might never have met Mack.'

There was a beat or two of silence.

'Why did you have a one-night stand with Mack's brother Fraser that night?' Lincoln asked. 'The night we ran into each other at that bar in Soho?'

Elodie shuffled away and sat upright and hugged her knees. 'I hope you're not going to go all double standards on me about having a one-night stand. You've had plenty.'

'I'm not denying it, but it seemed out of character for you.'

She gave him the side-eye. 'Were you jealous?'

'No.' His expression was masklike, except for a knot of tension in the lower quadrant of his jaw.

Elodie got off the bed and smoothed her hands over her satin wrap. 'It was awful, if you want to know…'

She wasn't sure why she was telling him about a night she would rather wipe from her memory for good. Running into Lincoln with his latest squeeze had rocked her far more than it should. The stunning young woman had been draped all over him, her adoration for him obvious for all to see. It shouldn't have upset Elodie one iota, but for some reason it had thrown her into a tailspin. His partner had looked *so* in love with him. The same way Elodie had once looked up at him—as if he was the only man in the world who could make her happy.

Her mind back then had run through a reel of thoughts—would he announce their engagement soon? Would they settle down and have the family he had once wanted with her?

To distract herself, she'd flirted outrageously with Fraser MacDiarmid, determined to show Lincoln she was completely and utterly over him, but it had backfired spectacularly a few months later.

Lincoln rose from the bed in a single movement and came over to her. 'Did he…hurt you?' A thread of anger underpinned his voice and his expression was a landscape of concern.

Elodie hugged her arms around her middle and gave him a stiff, no-teeth-showing smile. 'It was consensual but crappy sex.'

His eyes held hers. 'You didn't enjoy it?'

'If you're asking did I come, then, no, I didn't.'

Why are you telling him that?

But it seemed now she'd opened her mouth, she couldn't stop confessing the rest. She gave him a pointed look. 'It's your fault, you know. You've spoilt me for anyone else.'

A frown formed on his forehead. 'What do you mean?'

She blew out a long breath. 'I haven't enjoyed sex since we broke up.'

There was a weighted pause.

'Have there been many lovers?' Lincoln's tone was mild—casual, almost—and yet she sensed an undercurrent of avid interest he was trying his best to hide.

Elodie unwound her arms from around her middle. 'Not as many as I've led people to believe.' She speared a hand through the loose tresses of her hair and continued, 'I suppose that gives your male ego a massive boost? That I can't come with anyone else?'

His expression didn't register surprise, for hardly a muscle moved on his face, and yet she still suspected he was shocked. Deeply shocked. And why wouldn't he be? The press had documented her every move over the last seven years, linking her with various high-profile men. She had played to the cameras, using every opportunity to lift her profile. Some of the men she had had flings with—many she had not.

'Casual sex isn't for everybody.' His tone was as hard to read as his expression.

Elodie gave a mirthless laugh. 'You seem to do all right. As I recall, you didn't even wait a week before finding someone else after our breakup.'

Seeing him in a gossip magazine with an attractive partner within a week of their aborted wedding had struck at her heart like a closed-fist punch. If he had cared for her even a little, wouldn't he have waited just a while in case she changed her mind? But, no. He'd moved on so rapidly it had confirmed she had done the right thing in calling off their wedding. For if he had loved her wouldn't he have at least tried to change her mind rather than replace her?

Lincoln rolled his bottom lip over his top one in a contemplative gesture, his eyes still holding hers. After a long moment, he released a long-winded sigh. 'I didn't sleep with anyone for months after we split up.' His voice was low and rough around the edges.

Elodie stared at him, her heart skipping out of its normal rhythm. 'But…but I thought… *Really?*' She leaned on the word, suddenly desperate to know the truth. 'Why not? And why did you give everyone the impression you'd moved on so quickly?'

Lincoln looked down at the floor, where he was idly using the toe of his shoe to straighten the fringe of the Persian rug. When he raised his gaze back to hers his expression was still unreadable.

'I'd better let you get some sleep. We fly first thing in the morning.' He moved across to the door with long, purposeful strides.

'But wait,' Elodie said, following him, placing a hand on his arm before he could open the door to leave. She looked up into his enigmatic features, her mind whirling from what he'd told her. 'Was it because you were hoping I'd come back to you? You thought I might change my mind?'

He held her gaze in an unwavering lock for endless seconds, but there was no clue to what he was thinking. It was like trying to read the expression on a marble statue.

'Do you really think I would've taken you back?' he said at last, in a cynical tone that stung far more than it should.

Elodie kept her expression as masklike as his. She removed her hand from his arm and stepped back. 'No.'

The door closed behind him and she let out a rattling sigh.

Why would he if he hadn't loved her in the first place?

The journey to Valencia in Spain the following day took just over six hours door-to-door. Elodie spent most of it with her head buried in a collection of fashion magazines, determined to keep her distance, knowing that as soon as they were in Nina Smith's presence the charade of being a happily reunited loved-up couple would begin.

Lincoln seemed just as disinclined to talk—he had business papers in his briefcase and wore a preoccupied frown for most of the journey.

A car was waiting for them at the airport, with a young uniformed driver called Elonzo. *'Buenas tardes, Señor Lancaster.'* He smiled shyly at Elodie and added, *'Señora, mucho gusto.'*

'It's nice to meet you too,' Elodie said, with an answering smile that made the young man blush in spite of his olive complexion.

Lincoln helped Elodie into the car and they were soon on their way to the villa at Sagunto, about twenty minutes' drive from the airport. The sunshine was blindingly bright, the air warm in comparison to the chilly autumn weather back home.

'Have you been to Sagunto before?' Lincoln asked.

'No, but I've been to a few other places in Spain.

It's one of my favourite destinations. The people are so friendly, the food is great—and don't even get me started about the weather.'

Lincoln gave a lazy smile and laid his arm along the back of her seat. 'You've already won over one heart.' He nodded towards the young driver, who was shut off from them by a panel of glass for privacy. 'Let's hope Nina is as easy to win over.'

Elodie angled her head to look at him. 'You don't call her "Mum" now that your adoptive mother has passed away?'

He absently toyed with the loose strands of her hair, sending electrifying tingles down her back.

'I don't think it's appropriate. My adoptive mother will always be my mother, so too my father. They earned the titles by the love and care they gave me all those years.'

'Given you had such a nice childhood, I find it intriguing as to why you no longer want children yourself.'

His hand stopped playing with her hair and went back to resting along the back of her seat. A line of tension formed around his mouth. 'When my mother died I was thrown off course, as were my father and siblings. Pancreatic cancer took her so quickly. One minute she was well, the next she was critically ill, and she died within a few weeks. Dad went into a slump. I'd never seen him so low…' He released a long sigh and continued, 'Then I met you and I suddenly saw a future. A bright and happy future that would include kids and family life—the sort of family life my parents had given me.'

Elodie frowned, not sure she liked his reasons for wanting to marry her back then. They didn't seem to have anything to do with *her*. She could have been any suitable woman to fill the role as his wife and future mother of his children. He had liked what she represented—a beautiful wife to grace his home— but he hadn't loved *her*.

'But you don't hanker after that family life now?'

'Aiden and Sylvia are planning on having kids with their partners,' Lincoln said. 'My father will be thrilled to have a bunch of grandkids to dote on. I can concentrate on my work and on living life the way I prefer.'

'Footloose and fancy-free.' She didn't state it as a question but as a statement of fact. 'Once a playboy, always a playboy.'

Lincoln gave a mercurial smile. 'My inner playboy is on pause for the next six months.'

Elodie gave him a pointed look. 'Can I trust you on that?'

His eyes drifted to her mouth and then back to her gaze. 'The discipline will be good for me.'

CHAPTER SIX

Nina was waiting for them in the salon, where bright shafts of sunlight were coming in from the large windows, casting her in a golden, almost ethereal glow. She rose from the sofa and came towards them with both hands outstretched, her expression warm and welcoming.

'It is so lovely to meet you at last, my dear. Lincoln has told me so much about you.'

Elodie took the older woman's soft hands in hers and gave them a gentle squeeze. 'It's wonderful to meet you too. And lovely of you to have us stay with you for a couple of days.'

Nina kissed Elodie on both cheeks and then, releasing her hands, turned to Lincoln. Her eyes watered, as if she could barely believe he was really standing there in front of her. It touched Elodie to see the love in Nina's eyes.

'Lincoln, darling, thank you for bringing your beautiful wife to meet me. I know you're terribly busy, and I really do appreciate it.'

Lincoln enveloped his biological mother in a gentle

hug. It was as if he was worried he might break her. She was indeed a little thin, and had a frail air about her, but her eyes were sparking and clear.

'It's always good to see you. How have you been?'

Nina eased out of his hold with a crooked smile. 'So-so. Some days are better than others. But today is a good day.' She beamed at Elodie. 'Shall we have a drink to celebrate your marriage? Alita has made some sangria. We can go out to the terrace and enjoy the view.'

A short time later they were sitting under a large umbrella on the terrace with tall glasses of delicious and refreshing sangria in front of them. Elodie couldn't take her eyes off the stunning vista in front of her: ancient Roman ruins, including an outdoor theatre, interspersed with lush green hills and the port of Sagunto in the distance.

'Wow, it's so lovely…' She put her glass down before she was tempted to drain it. The last thing she wanted to do was get tipsy in front of Nina. But then, being here with Lincoln, especially with him sitting so close and holding one of her hands, was enough to make her feel drunk.

'It's my happy place,' Nina said, with a smile that encompassed Lincoln as well.

'Have you lived here long?' Elodie asked, reaching for one of the marinated olives on the tapas plate on the table.

'Two years,' Nina said and, glancing lovingly at Lincoln, added, 'Lincoln bought the villa for me as a birthday gift soon after we met. So very generous of him.'

Elodie put the pit of her olive on the little dish set on the table for such a purpose. She knew all about his generosity. He had bought her expensive gifts in the past—the missing engagement ring being a case in point. It still irked her that he didn't believe she had taken it back to his house. But if he hadn't found it, surely his housekeeper had? It couldn't have disappeared unless someone had stolen it—someone else who'd come into the house that day. Her new engagement ring was even more expensive, but she realised with a jolt that it was his trust she valued the most. That, to her, was priceless. Would he ever give it to her?

'I guess he missed a lot of your birthdays, so it was his way of making up for it.'

Nina's smile faded and she sighed and looked away into the distance. 'Yes, a lot of birthdays…'

Lincoln released Elodie's hand and stood, bending down to drop a light kiss to the top of her head. 'If you will excuse me? I'm going to have a chat to Elonzo about some maintenance that needs doing. I'll see you at dinner.'

Elodie waited until he had walked down the stairs from the terrace that led into the expansive gardens below before she turned back to look at Nina. 'It must have been very difficult to give him up all those years ago.'

Nina's eyes shimmered and her chin gave a distinct wobble. She reached for her glass of sangria but didn't drink from it. Her fingers moved up and down the frosted glass in a reflective manner.

'I wanted to keep him so much. It tore my heart out to give him up. But I was young and left reeling after the death of Lincoln's father. He was killed in a motorcycle accident on his way to see me when I was four months pregnant. I didn't have my family's support. They were deeply religious, and I knew bringing a born-out-of-wedlock child into the family would have a negative impact on the child in the long run.'

She glanced at Elodie, her expression pained.

'I decided to give Lincoln away to give him the best chance in life. I always thought I did the right thing, but when I met him a couple of years ago…' She gave a long sigh and continued, 'I could see he wasn't happy. Oh, he was successful, and wealthy beyond belief, and he'd had a good childhood thanks to his wonderful adoptive parents… But in himself… No. Not happy.'

She looked into Elodie's eyes.

'I blamed myself for that. I tortured myself with it. But now he is back with you he will be content at last. I know it in my heart of hearts.'

Elodie painted a smile on her face, feeling her own heart cramping in her chest at the deception she was complicit in. She was surprised Nina couldn't see through it—but then, didn't people who wanted something so badly see it even when it wasn't there? Nina wanted Lincoln's happiness more than anything else in the world. She believed that happiness and fulfilment could be achieved through being reunited with his runaway bride—*her*.

'I'm surprised you're not angry with me for walking out on our wedding day seven years ago.'

Nina put her glass down and took one of Elodie's hands, holding her gaze once more. 'I didn't know you or Lincoln back then. But I can see you love him now. That's all that matters, yes?'

Elodie looked down at their joined hands, her emotions in turmoil. How could she blatantly lie to a dying woman? It seemed morally wrong to continue the pretence. She sensed a bond with Nina…a connection that was beyond explanation. Or was it because they both loved Lincoln?

'The thing is… I'm not sure he loves me the way I love him.'

There was a silence broken only by the rustling of leaves as a breeze passed by and the tweeting of birds in the shrubbery. In the distance, a motor scooter revved and whined as it went up one of the winding hills leading to the ruins of a castle.

Nina gently stroked the back of Elodie's hand. 'You've always loved him, yes? Even when you called off the wedding seven years ago?'

Elodie met the older woman's gaze, deciding to be honest not just to Lincoln's mother but also to herself. 'I was frightened I was going to lose myself in our relationship back then. Lincoln is so driven and focussed—success is everything to him. And I knew it would be hard to make my own mark on the world while living in his shadow.'

She pulled her hand away and laid it on her lap, curling up her fingers so her engagement and wedding rings caught the light.

'I saw it happen to my mother when my sister developed a nut allergy. She gave up everything to be at home with Elspeth. My dad walked out when we were six, leaving her with the burden of taking care of two little kids, one of whom could die at any moment from anaphylactic shock.' She let out a sigh and continued, 'Mum didn't just lose her career, she lost her potential to be the person she wanted to be. The person she thought she *would* be. I didn't want that to happen to me.'

'We all make choices we have to live with.' Nina gave a wistful smile. 'I've revisited my choice about giving up Lincoln so many times. I wasn't lucky enough to have any other children. I thought I was being punished for not keeping him. Not a day went past that I didn't think of him, wondering what he looked like, what he sounded like, what he was good at and so on. I'd walk past young men in the street and wonder if one of them could be him. I positively ached to find him, but I couldn't summon up the courage until two years ago—I was too terrified that he wouldn't want anything to do with me. I was blessed that he did. And then I realised he wasn't truly happy. I wondered if it was my fault he found it hard to express love because of being relinquished as a baby. You know...what if the bonding issue was ruined for him way back then?'

'But you did what you thought was the best for

him at the time. And he had a happy childhood. His parents loved him as their own.'

'I know, and I'll be forever grateful for that. But, like me, you now have to get to a point where you forgive and accept yourself and your choices. You did what you thought was right at the time by calling off the wedding. And now, like me, you've been lucky enough to get a second chance. Not everyone gets that.'

Elodie gave an answering smile touched by melancholy. 'I guess you're right.'

She might be able to forgive herself, but would Lincoln ever do so? That was the question she had no idea how to answer.

Elodie left Nina soon after, so the older woman could have a rest before dinner. The youngish housekeeper-cum-cook, Alita, escorted Elodie to the suite she had prepared with obvious pride. She opened the door of the bedroom on the first floor with a wide smile, her eyes sparkling as if she had binge-watched romantic movies and television shows for most of her life.

'Welcome to the honeymoon suite, Señora Lancaster. Elonzo brought up your luggage earlier. I hope you will be comfortable.'

'Thank you.'

Elodie stepped into the graciously decorated suite, trying not to notice the king-sized bed made up with snowy-white linen and the array of blood-red rose petals artfully scattered on top. The bed might be big enough to accommodate two people, but when those two people were her and Lincoln what would happen? His hands-off rule was going to be tested to the limit, that was what. And her self-control—never good around him at the best of times—was going to be challenged like never before.

Elodie heard the door close behind her as Alita left and let out a long, ragged breath. She moved across the wide expanse of floor to the bed, picturing Lincoln's dark head on the pillow next to hers.

Something in her belly turned over and her heart skipped a beat. She had fought for years to rid her mind of the erotic memories of being in his arms. The pleasure he'd evoked, the intense feelings he'd stirred in her like no one else. But she only had to close her eyes to recall the sensual glide of his hands along her naked flesh. His touch had sent fireworks through her blood each and every time. How could she share a bed with him and not want him?

The door opened again and she turned to see Lincoln standing there with an inscrutable expression. He shut the door with a definitive click that seemed overly loud in the silence. 'Everything all right?'

Elodie folded her arms and pursed her lips. 'The honeymoon suite has been lovingly prepared for us by Nina's delightful young housekeeper.'

He came further into the room and tossed his phone on the end of the bed. 'I'm sure we'll manage to keep our hands off each other.'

She angled her head at him. 'You think?'

He gave an indolent smile and walked over to where she was standing, stopping just in front of her. Close enough for her to see the green and blue flecks in his eyes and the dark bottomless circles of his pupils.

'What? Are you worried you won't be able to keep your hands off me?'

Elodie unfolded her arms and placed them on his chest. 'I have a feeling you *want* me to put my hands on you. You want it very much.'

Her voice came out as a throaty whisper and she felt her pulse kicking up its pace at his nearness. The salt and citrus smell of him teased her senses, and the hard muscles of his chest beneath her hands reminded her of the potent power of his male body. She could almost feel it rising in the small space between their bodies—the arousal he couldn't hide or deny.

She pressed herself against the swollen heat of his body, relishing the potent length of him responding to her in spite of his rules. There were no rules strong enough to contain the lust they felt for each other. She could feel it in the air like a third presence in the room. A throbbing invisible energy that drew them together as powerfully as a magnet to metal.

Lincoln's eyes darkened and he drew in a sharp-sounding breath, his hands going to her upper arms in a hold that was on the wrong side of gentle. But she didn't care if he left fingerprints on her flesh. She wanted him. All of him.

'You're playing a dangerous game.'

His tone was rough and deep, his fingers momentarily tightening on her arms.

'What's so dangerous about doing what we do so

well, hmm? Or have you forgotten how good we were together?'

His hooded gaze went to her mouth, lingered there for a pulsing moment. 'No, damn you, I haven't forgotten.'

He brought his mouth down on hers in an explosive kiss that sent a rush of heat through her body. His hands left her upper arms to move around her, crushing her closer to him, so close she could feel the hardened ridge of his erection. A frisson passed through her—a delicious frisson that made the hairs on her head stand on end and a pool of molten heat form in her core.

He backed her up against the nearest wall, his mouth still clamped to hers. She arched her spine in a desperate quest for more intimate friction, and gasped when one of his hands lifted her dress to her hips. His hand gliding along her bare thigh sent another wave of intense heat through her core. Damp heat that smouldered and steamed and simmered in secret.

Lincoln's mouth moved from hers to kiss the ultra-sensitive skin below her ear, the movement of his lips sending shivers cascading down her spine. He moved lower to the skin of her neck, and then her décolletage, the caresses light but no less tantalising. His hand slid further up her thigh to the edge of her knickers. Fervid excitement sent her pulse-rate soaring and her stomach swooped.

'Oh, God, *yes...*' she gasped against his mouth.

He traced the seam of her body through the lace

of her knickers, his intimate touch making her grind against his hand, desperate to assuage the burning ache of her flesh. He pushed her knickers to one side and his mouth came back down hard on hers, his tongue mimicking the flickering action of his fingers. The tension built in her to snapping point, a rush of sensation barrelling through her until she was swept off into the abyss on a tumultuous tide of pleasure.

Elodie clung to his tall frame, not sure her trembling legs would hold her upright as the aftershocks rumbled through her body. But, as intensely pleasurable as her orgasm had been, she knew she couldn't afford to let him think there was anything more than animal lust between them.

There wasn't and never could be.

She had loved him once, with a consuming, overwhelming love that had almost caused her to give up everything she had planned for her life. But she had come to her senses just in time.

If she had married him when she was twenty-one she would have been little more than a trophy wife. A beautiful woman who would grace his home and bear his children and then be pushed aside when she lost her looks or he got bored with her. She wouldn't have built her career to what it was today. She wouldn't have built her profile to the point where she could use it to fulfil her dream of producing her own designs.

Lincoln had never told her he loved her. She had pressed him a few times, but he had never said those three little magical words. And what was the point of hoping he might say them in the future? He had been blatantly honest about his reasons for marrying her. She was only back in his life because he wanted to give his dying mother end-of-life peace.

There was no other reason.

Elodie straightened her clothes with a sultry smile. 'You certainly haven't lost your touch.' She tiptoed her fingers down to the waistband of his chinos. 'Let's see if I've lost mine, shall we?'

Lincoln's hand captured hers in a firm hold, his expression unreadable. 'No.'

She arched her brows in a cynical manner, determined not so show how much his rejection hurt her. She pulled her hand out of his and opened and closed her fingers, her skin tingling from the heat of his touch. 'You really are serious about those rules of yours, aren't you?'

'I am.'

Elodie shifted her mouth from side to side in a musing way. 'May I ask why?'

'I told you—it will make it a lot easier to dissolve our marriage when the six months is up.'

He moved to the other side of the room, taking his jacket from where it was lying over the back of a chair and moving towards the built-in wardrobe. He slid one of the mirrored doors back and took a coat hanger from the rack. He hung his jacket on it, then placed it in the wardrobe and closed the door again. His actions were precise, methodical, as though the task helped him process his thoughts.

He turned and faced her again, with a light of determination in his gaze that struck a chord of unease in her. 'I don't want any lasting mistakes from our temporary union.'

Elodie frowned, in spite of her determination to act cool and unmoved by his stern composure and stance. 'What do you mean by "lasting mistakes"?'

His eyes bored into hers. 'Are you currently using contraception?'

'Of course.'

A low-dose pill was her only option at the moment, because she had struggled to find one that didn't affect her mood. Not that she was good at remembering to take it regularly. But she'd figured that since she hadn't exactly been putting herself 'out there' since her ill-fated hook-up with Fraser MacDiarmid, it was the best alternative. And since Lincoln was so adamant their marriage was to be on paper only—well, what did it matter if it didn't have the same reliability as other methods?

Lincoln held her gaze for a pulsing moment, then his eyes drifted to her mouth and he sucked in an audible breath. 'We'll have to share the bed or Alita and Nina will suspect something is up.'

Elodie gave him a playful smile, sensing he was struggling to keep to his own rules. It gave her a sense of feminine power that sent a thrill through her flesh. He wanted her, but his fight was not with her but with himself.

'Do you want to toss for which side to sleep on? I seem to remember you like being on the right—or have you changed since we last—?'

'The right is still my preference.'

She made a little snorting noise. 'That figures.'

'Why?'

'Because you always like to be right.'

A crooked smile formed on his lips. 'So do you.'

Elodie shrugged in a nonchalant manner, and went to the dressing table where she had left her cosmetics. She picked up her cleanser and then sat on the velvet-covered chair. She caught his eye in the mirror. 'What?'

Lincoln came over and laid his hands on the tops of her shoulders, still holding her gaze in the mirror. 'I haven't really thanked you properly for agreeing to all this.'

There was a different quality to his tone—a softer, warmer note that made her heart suddenly contract.

'All this?'

'Pretending to be in love and happily married. It means the world to Nina to see us reunited.'

Elodie placed one of her hands over his, where it was resting on her shoulder. 'I really like her. It's so sad that she has so little time left with you…especially as you only found each other a couple of years ago.'

One of his hands began playing with the long tresses of her hair in an absent fashion. His touch sent shivers dancing over her scalp and down her spine.

'Life isn't always fair, but we have to deal with it.' His hand fell away from her hair, the other from her shoulder.

Elodie spun around on the chair and craned her neck to look up at him. 'How will you deal with it? Her death, I mean?'

Lincoln let out a long breath and rubbed a hand over his face. 'The same way I coped with losing my adoptive mother.'

She raised her eyebrows. 'By trying to rush into marrying a woman you barely knew and didn't even love?'

There was a beat or two of silence.

Lincoln continued to hold her gaze, but his was screened—like a blacked-out window in an abandoned building. There was a muscle near the corner of his mouth that twitched once or twice, as if he couldn't decide whether to give a rueful smile or grind his teeth, and then he released a long sigh.

'I wish I'd searched for her earlier. I lost her as a baby and now I'm going to lose her again. When we're only just getting to know one another. She's filled the hole my adoptive mother left behind, but I'm conscious of the time ticking away. Every day that goes by is a day closer to losing her. It's... torturous, to be honest.'

'Oh, Lincoln, I'm so sorry. It must be hard for both of you.'

He gave a stiff movement of his lips that passed for a dismissive smile. 'We'd better dress for dinner. Nina likes to dine early as she gets tired. I'll leave you to get ready in private.'

Elodie watched him stride away to the door of their suite. 'Lincoln?'

His hand had almost reached the doorknob, but he lowered it to his side and turned to face her, his expression guarded. 'Yes?'

His tone was clipped, with an edge of impatience, which only made her all the more determined to get close to him. He had lowered his guard enough to tell her about his sadness over the prospect of losing Nina. What else might he reveal if she encouraged him to be vulnerable with her? Would getting close to him physically unlock more of his emotional armour? What if the Lincoln she'd been engaged to in the past was not the *real* Lincoln? What if, like her, he had kept back a part of himself he allowed few people, if any, to see?

'You don't have to leave while I get ready. We've dressed and undressed in front of each other before— heaps of times. And we can take turns using the bathroom.' A smile played at the corners of her mouth and she added, 'I promise I won't peek.'

The line of his mouth remained tight, but his eyes darkened. 'I'm going for a walk. I'll be back in half an hour.'

He walked out and closed the door with a firm click that sounded as definitive as a punctuation mark.

Lincoln went for a brisk walk through the gardens to get himself back in line. The more time he spent with Elodie alone, the harder it was to resist her. She was flirting outrageously with him, and he would be lying if he said he didn't enjoy every moment of her playful behaviour.

He did. Too much. Way too much.

But it wasn't just the playful flirting that got to him. She had revealed more about herself than she ever had in the past, and so had he. This new emotional connection between them was strange…foreign to him…because he always kept people at a distance. And keeping Elodie at a distance was supposed to be his top priority.

But she was making it near impossible to keep his hands off her—especially as he remembered all too well how clever those little hands of hers could be. How hot and tempting her soft mouth. Kissing her had almost blown the top of his head off. And the passion that flared between them was getting harder and harder to control.

Her cheeky bend-the-rules personality had always appealed to him—mostly because his nature tended to lean towards the colour-between-the-lines conservative. She evoked in his staider personality a recklessness that was exciting to indulge. She made his flesh sing when she touched him. Her lips had set his alight and he could still taste the fresh sweetness of her. It was like a drug he had forgotten how much he craved. One taste and he was addicted all over again.

But their marriage had a short timeline, and he was adamant there would be no casualties in the aftermath. As far as he was concerned this was a business deal like any other. Emotions were not required, and in fact only blurred the boundaries. And he needed boundaries when it came to Elodie.

Firm, impenetrable boundaries.

Lincoln stood for a moment, looking at the view of the ruins of Sagunto Castle. The fortress-style castle had a history going back two thousand years. His history with Elodie was much shorter. And while the fortress he had built around himself was not quite in crumbling ruins, he would still have to be careful to keep it secure.

But... But...

A persistent voice kept niggling at him. What if he indulged himself with a little tweak of the rules? After all, he had always kept his emotions out of his sex life. Sex was a physical experience he enjoyed on a regular basis, with like-minded women who played by the same rules. No strings, no promises, no commitment other than for a brief interlude of mutual pleasure.

The pleasure he and Elodie had experienced together in the past was something he couldn't eradicate from his mind or indeed from his body. The memory of possessing her, the slick, wet tightness of her body and her passionate response to him, was something he had never been able to recreate to quite the same degree with anyone else. In fact, for years he'd had trouble having sex without his mind drifting to her.

Maybe these six months would be the antidote to his obsession with her. He could finally move on with his life once he had ruled a thick black line under them as a couple.

End of story.

No sequel.

No reruns.

Finished.

Elodie was doing the final touches to her make-up when Lincoln came back to their suite. She squinted one eye to apply her volume-enhancing mascara. 'The bathroom's free.' She blinked a couple of times and then dabbed the wand back into the container. 'I hope what I'm wearing is okay. Not too OTT?'

Lincoln would have preferred to see her naked, but decided to keep that to himself. The hot pink dress she was wearing should have clashed with her red-gold hair and creamy complexion, but somehow she made everything look stunning on her.

'You look great.'

He moved further into the room, resisting the temptation to touch her. He could smell her perfume—a rich, exotic blend of flowers and spice that teased his nostrils and tantalised his senses. Her hair was piled up in a makeshift bun that somehow managed to looked casual and elegant at the same time. But then, that was Elodie to a tee. She would look glamorous without a scrap of make-up on and dressed in a rubbish bin liner.

She reached for her lip-gloss and leaned closer to the mirror to apply it. He couldn't tear his eyes off her plump lips as she painted the glistening colour on her mouth. She pressed her lips softly together and then glanced at him in the mirror, a mercurial smile forming, her blue eyes sparkling like the diamond droplet earrings dangling from her ears.

'Nice walk?'

'Nice enough.'

She picked up a soft brush and dusted some highlighter down the slope of her nose. 'Still hot outside?'

'Yes.'

But not as hot as in here, Lincoln wanted to say, but didn't.

Heat was pooling in his groin—a fiery heat that bloomed and flared like wildfire. If ever there was a time for a cold shower, this was it. He went into the en suite bathroom and closed the door, but even in there he was surrounded by the alluring, bewitching scent of her.

There were wet towels hanging haphazardly over the rail and he suppressed a wry smile. It was certainly an improvement from her leaving them on the floor, as she had so often in the past. He had argued about it with her numerous times, but he had never managed to housetrain her. He wondered now why he'd bothered. Of course, these days Elodie had a team of people picking up after her. She had personal assistants and make-up artists and hair stylists who were at her beck and call, catering to her every whim.

Lincoln had to make sure he didn't become one of them.

CHAPTER SEVEN

ELODIE WALKED DOWN to the dining room with Lincoln a short time later. He was dressed in a casual suit with an open-necked white shirt that brought out the olive tan of his skin. She had briefly left their suite while he showered and changed, not sure she could trust herself not to melt at his feet if he came out dressed in only a towel slung around his lean hips.

Lincoln's arm slipped around her waist as they entered the dining room.

Nina looked up from her seat with a warm smile. 'You both look so good together—like movie stars or something. I love those earrings, Elodie. Did Lincoln give them to you?'

Elodie flicked one of her earrings with her finger. 'No, I was given them by a lingerie designer a couple of years ago.'

'It must be an exciting life…travelling the world and modelling lovely things,' Nina said.

'Yes, well…it's kind of lost its appeal, to be honest,' Elodie said, as Lincoln pulled out her chair for her. She flashed a smile of thanks to him and returned her gaze to Nina. 'I'm pursuing a new career now.'

'Lincoln told me you're an aspiring dress designer. How wonderfully creative. Maybe you could design something for me...' A flicker of something passed over her face and she continued in a subdued tone, 'Not that I could give you much time to do so, given my diagnosis.'

Elodie reached for the older woman's hand and gave it a gentle squeeze, her own eyes watering. So much for never showing her emotions, but something about Lincoln's biological mum's situation tore at her heartstrings.

'I'm sorry to hear you're so ill. Life can be unfair. Is there nothing that can be done? Nothing at all?'

Nina patted Elodie's hand in a resigned manner. 'There have been so many treatments and experiments and drugs, but I'm something of a mystery to my doctors. I get the feeling they don't know what to do with me now. They've run out of options. I've come to terms with it, more or less. But it will be sad not living long enough to meet my grandchildren... I would have loved that more than anything...' She gave a deep sigh and stretched her lips into a smile. 'But let's not be maudlin. I have much to be grateful for and I count each day as a bonus—especially now you two are back together.'

Elodie wasn't game to look in Lincoln's direction and kept her gaze focussed on Nina's. 'I'd love to design you a dress—in fact, a complete wardrobe of outfits. You might as well make the most of the time you have left. And there are such things as miracles. It's good to have some hope, I guess. That's better than giving up, right?'

Nina's smile was so motherly and affectionate it made Elodie's heart all but explode with emotion.

'Sweet child. I can see why my son fell so hard for you. Design away, my dear. I will be proud to wear every item.'

Elodie was so inspired to get to work on some outfits for Nina that she barely touched the delicious food placed before her during the meal. Her mind was buzzing, and colours and fabric designs were swirling about in her head as she planned a bright and colourful collection.

Finally, the meal came to an end and Nina bade them goodnight and retired to her quarters.

Lincoln picked up his still half-full wine glass and gestured to Elodie to do the same. 'Come out to the terrace for a while. It's a little early to go to bed.'

Elodie raised her eyebrows. Was he prolonging the time before the moment they'd have to go upstairs to share the suite? Surely he wasn't...*nervous*?

She curved her lips into a teasing smile. 'Since when is it too early for us to go to bed? I seem to remember us having quite a number of early nights in the past.'

A glinting light appeared in his gaze. 'That was never the problem between us, was it? The sex?'

She glanced over her shoulder to see Alita, the young housekeeper, hovering in the doorway, waiting to clear the room. 'Thanks for a lovely meal, Alita.'

'You're most welcome, *señora.*'

Elodie turned back to Lincoln. 'The terrace sounds like a good idea.'

And, picking up her own glass, she followed him out through the French doors to where a full moon was shining.

The shift of location gave her a moment to reflect on their past relationship. Making love with Lincoln had always been phenomenal. From their very first time it had showed her a world of sensuality and pleasure she hadn't experienced with anyone else before. But while it had been wonderful in every way, it had also covered up the tiny cracks in their relationship that had been there right from the start. Fine cracks that had developed into the deep fissures she had ignored until the day of their wedding, when she hadn't been able to ignore them any longer.

They hadn't communicated other than through sex. And making love was not a good substitute for effective communication. Perfect strangers could have good sex. She had never been able to share her doubts and fears and insecurities with him and he had never shared his—if he'd had any, that was.

'Actually, I think it was a big part of the problem.'

Lincoln leaned against the stone balustrade with his glass in one hand. 'What do you mean?' There was an edge of guardedness in his tone.

Elodie moved across the terrace to stand within half a metre of him and placed her glass of wine on the balustrade. The last thing she needed was more alcohol to loosen her tongue. 'I think we used the chemistry we had together as a distraction from… other things.'

'What other things?'

She half turned to look up at him, but the moonlight coming from behind him had cast his features into an unreadable shadow. 'When we argued over something, we used sex to clear the air rather than sitting down and talking through stuff. Talking about why we had argued in the first place.' She licked her lips and continued, 'It was a pattern we drifted into from the start. Fight and have make-up sex. We never resolved the underlying issue.'

'Which was?'

'We knew each other physically, but not emotionally.'

Lincoln moved so that he was looking out at the moonlit view, his forehead creased in a frown. 'I'm not saying you were totally to blame for our breakup,' he said. 'I didn't like how you went about it, that's all.'

His grip on his wine glass was so tight, she was worried it might break.

'You should've told me you weren't happy,' he added.

'But that's my point. We never *talked* about things. We never got that far. You were always busy chasing your next big deal, becoming more and more successful, as if that was the only thing that really mattered to you. I was nothing more than an ornament to you. A plaything you enjoyed having at your disposal. I was never your equal.'

He put his glass on the balustrade too, as if he too

was worried it might shatter under his grip. He turned to look at her, his expression still in shadow. 'Why did you feel you couldn't talk to me?'

The quality of his tone had changed—become softer, less defensive, more concerned.

Elodie blew out a soft breath. 'I don't know…' She gave a little shrug and continued, 'Maybe because I didn't think you would understand how important having a career was to me. I got the impression you wanted me to be a homemaker, like your adoptive mother, not a career woman. It scared me because that's what happened to my mum. She gave up everything to take care of Elspeth when she got sick. Then my dad left when we were six and poor Mum was left with nothing. No career, no money and no support other than the pittance he sent only because he was legally required to, not because he wanted to. No wonder she turned into a nervous wreck who never seemed to notice she had two children, not just one. I didn't just lose my dad when he left—I lost my mother too.'

There was a silence.

Lincoln reached out with one of his hands to brush a loose tendril of hair away from her face. 'I'm sorry. I didn't realise how hard that must've been for you. I knew your father was a bit of a lost cause, but I didn't know you felt pushed aside by your mother as well.'

Elodie grimaced. 'It's not really her fault. She did her best, and Elspeth was so sick a couple of times that losing her was a very real possibility. I learned to get attention in other ways—not always sensible ways, mind you…but, hey, it worked until it didn't.'

Lincoln's hand moved to capture one of hers, his fingers warm and gentle as he cradled it as if it was a baby bird. 'I guess none of us get out of childhood without a few issues, but it must have been terrifying to think you might lose your twin. You're still close, yes?'

Elodie smiled a little wistfully. 'Yes, she's amazing—especially now she's in love. She's really blossomed. Mack's been wonderful for her and she for him.' Her smile faded and she added, 'But I guess now Mack will be her go-to person, not me.'

Lincoln began an idle stroking over the back of her hand with his thumb, his gaze still trained on hers. 'I'm sure she'll always have a special place in her life for you.'

'Are you close to your siblings? And your father?'

He looked down at their joined hands for a moment, a slight frown pulling at his brow. 'I'm probably not as attentive a son and big brother as I should be. I'm always busy with work and travelling and so on.' He looked back at her and gave a rueful smile. 'Sylvia is always nagging me to make more time for family gatherings, but it's not the same without Mum.'

There was a thread of sadness in his tone that made her realise how deeply he still missed his adoptive mother. And now he had to face the prospect of losing his biological mother. Was it any wonder he would do anything—including marrying *her*—to make Nina's last days as peaceful and happy as possible?

Elodie found herself moving closer to him, one of her hands going to rest against his chest, the other reaching up to stroke the side of his lean jaw. 'Oh, Lincoln, I'm so sorry you lost her. And now you have to face losing Nina too.'

Lincoln settled his hands on her hips, his expression cast in grave lines. 'The thing that gets me is not knowing for sure when it will be. She looks fine at the moment—you'd hardly think anything was wrong. And yet on another day she can go down quickly and need to be in bed all day.'

'But you said the doctors told you no more than three or four months?'

He let out a serrated sigh. 'That was what they said the last time I spoke to them. It's not a long time, is it?'

'No, but I read this saying once: even the dying are still living. It's important that Nina gets to do all the things she wants to do. I meant what I said about designing a new wardrobe of clothes for her. I was mentally preparing sketches during dinner. I can't wait to get started.'

Lincoln smiled and lifted one of his hands to brush her cheek with his fingers. 'She's quite taken with you. I knew she would be.'

Elodie chewed at her lip for a moment. 'I can't help feeling a bit compromised, though. I mean, pretending we're madly in love when we can barely stand the sight of each other…'

He eased up her chin and locked gazes with her, his expression serious. 'Do you hate me that much?'

The problem was that she didn't hate him at all. She had the opposite problem—she was madly, deeply, crazily in love with him. Had she ever *not* been in love with him? She had tried to deny it, hide it, disguise it, but while it was possible to hide it from him, she couldn't hide it from herself. And hadn't Nina noticed it too? The older woman had intuitively sensed the feelings Elodie was keeping under lock and key for fear of being rejected.

Elodie gazed into the darkness of his eyes and tried to ignore the fluttering of her pulse. Tried to ignore the sensual pull of his body, the magnetic energy that drew her even closer until her hips were flush against his. 'No… I don't hate you…' Her voice came as a whisper, as soft as the night breeze currently playing with the tendrils of her hair.

He framed her face in his hands, his gaze still trained on hers. 'It would be easier if you did, you know…' His voice was as rough as the stone balustrade that held their wine glasses.

'Why?'

'Because then I wouldn't be tempted to do this.'

He lowered his mouth to hers in a long, drugging kiss that sent shivers racing up and down her spine like electrodes. His tongue entered her mouth with erotic intent, the glide and stroke of it against hers sending her senses haywire.

He made a groaning sound and drew her even closer, wrapping his arms around her. He angled his head to deepen the kiss, and a warm rush of longing almost overwhelmed her in its intensity. Kissing him wasn't enough. She wanted to feel his thick, hard presence where she needed it the most.

She moved against him, signalling her need, and he sucked in a harsh breath and kissed her more firmly, as if only just managing to stay in control.

After a few breathless moments, he lifted his mouth off hers, his eyes glazed with lust. 'About those rules…'

Elodie stepped up on tiptoe and planted another playful kiss to his lips. 'Don't tell me you've changed your mind about your silly old rules?'

He gave a lopsided smile and cupped the curves of her bottom in his hands, holding her against the pounding heat of his aroused body. 'Then I won't tell you. I'll show you instead.'

He scooped her up in his arms, and even though she gave a token squeak of protest continued carrying her through the French doors and all the way up the stairs to their suite.

Once they were inside their bedroom, he let her slide down the length of his body to the floor. Every deliciously sexy ridge of his toned body teased hers into a frenzy of want. Need clawed through her tingling flesh, making her wonder how she had gone seven years without feeling anywhere near this height of sensual awareness.

Lincoln crushed her mouth beneath his, the passionate pressure of his lips and the gliding thrust of his tongue into her mouth only ramping up her desire.

He raised his mouth barely a millimetre above

hers, his breath mingling intimately with hers. 'No one turns me on quite like you do.'

Elodie combed her fingers through his hair, barely able to take her eyes off his mouth. How could a man's mouth—this man's mouth—create such a firestorm of need in her body?

'I hate to boost your ego too much, but it's the same for me. I want you even though my head tells me it's a mistake to get involved again.'

He stroked his thumb over her bottom lip, his touch sending tingles straight from her mouth to her core. 'It's only for six months. It's not like we're making any promises beyond that.'

And there was the kicker for her. The time frame. The temporary nature of their marriage. So different from what he had proposed seven years ago. He had once offered her for ever. This time he had only offered for now.

And yet… And yet how could she not accept the new terms? She had not truly moved on from him, in spite of all her efforts. Maybe six months of living and sleeping together as man and wife would help her reframe their relationship. Help her to see it for what it was and always had been—nothing more than a stunning physical chemistry that would eventually burn itself out.

Elodie painted a smile on her lips—a fake smile that pulled at her mouth like too-tight stitches. 'You mean we're not going to fall in love with each other? That's still against the rules, right?'

A flicker of something passed through his hooded

gaze, like a blink-and-you'd-miss-it movement in a deeply shadowed forest. 'Do you think it's likely?' he asked.

'You mean for me or for you?'

'For you.'

Elodie kept her eyes focussed on the sculptured perfection of his mouth rather than meet the probing intensity of his gaze. Of course he wouldn't consider himself in any danger of falling in love with her. He hadn't before, so why would he now? He loved how she looked. He was in lust with her. Was he even capable of romantic love?

'Anything's a possibility, I guess.' She brought her gaze back to his with a carefree smile. 'But what has love got to do with red-hot lust, hey? Not much.'

Lincoln brought his mouth down to within a millimetre or two of hers. 'Speaking of lust…' He brushed her lips with a kiss that made her hungry for more. 'Do you have any idea of how much I want you right now?'

She nestled closer, delighting in the proud bulge of his erection. Her inner core tightened in anticipation. The walls of her womanhood were already slick with moisture. 'I think I've got a fair idea.'

She nibbled at the edge of his mouth with teasing little nibbles that she followed up with a sweep of her tongue. He groaned deep in his throat and grasped her by the hips, bringing her even closer.

'I want to go slowly,' he said in a husky tone.

'Don't you freaking dare…' Elodie pulled his head down so his mouth came back to set fire to hers.

CHAPTER EIGHT

ELODIE WOKE FROM a deep, blissful sleep to find Lincoln had left the bed. She glanced at the bedside clock and frowned. It was three in the morning. She pushed back the covers and slipped on her wrap, tying the ties around her waist. There was no light on in the bathroom, but the doors leading out to the balcony were open, for she could see the billowing of the silk curtains as the night breeze stirred them. She pushed the curtains aside to find Lincoln standing against the balustrade with his back to her. He was wearing his underwear but the rest of him was naked.

'Lincoln?'

He turned and smiled at her. 'Sorry. Did I wake you?'

'Not really.' She went over to where he was standing and touched him on the arm. 'Can't you sleep?'

He picked up her hand from where it was resting on his arm and brought it up to his mouth, his eyes still holding hers. He kissed the ends of her fingers, one by one, his touch sending tremors of pleasure through her body.

'I guess I've got used to spending the night alone.'

Elodie frowned. 'Alone? I don't understand… You mean you don't spend the night with any of your… your lovers?'

Lincoln released her hand and turned back to look at the moonlit view. His hands gripped the balustrade and even in the low light she could see the straining of the tendons in the backs of his hands. 'I prefer not to.'

Elodie stared at him for a long moment, trying to get her head around this latest revelation. *He no longer spent the whole night with a lover.* Then she recalled that he had said he hadn't been with anyone for months after their breakup, in spite of the photo she had seen in the press the week after she'd jilted him. The photo that had cut at her like a flick knife, making her hate him for moving on so quickly.

She hadn't realised until she saw the photo how much she had wanted him to come after her, to fight for her, to beg her to come back to him. To reassure her that he cared about her, that he wanted to be with her, that even, by some miracle, he loved her.

But he had done none of that.

And because of that damn photo she hadn't made any effort to contact him other than the brief note of apology she had left on the hall table with the engagement ring—which, of course, he claimed he hadn't got.

'Lincoln…you said the other day you didn't sleep with anyone for months after we broke up. Why was that?'

His expression was as screened as the moon was

just then by a passing cloud. 'Don't go reading too much into it.'

'But why did you actively encourage me—and the rest of the world when it comes to that—to believe you'd moved on to someone else the very next week?'

'Why would that upset you? You were the one who jilted me. You made it clear we were over. More than clear.'

Elodie shifted her gaze from his and rolled her top lip over her bottom one, a frown still pulling at her forehead. 'I know I had no right to be upset. I guess I thought you might…try and talk me round.'

He gave a short bark of incredulous laughter. 'Really? You mean come crawling on my hands and knees, begging you to come back to me? Shows how little you knew me back then.'

Her shoulders went down on a heavy sigh. 'Yes, well…that works both ways, doesn't it?'

Lincoln glanced at her, his expression still inscrutable. But then he sighed and raked a hand through his hair, before dropping it back by his side. 'Was there anything I could've said to get you to change your mind back then?'

His tone had lost its sharp, mocking edge and become deeper, almost gentle. Elodie forced a smile, not sure she wanted to reveal any more than she already had. It was funny, but she could parade in the skimpiest lingerie and swimwear on catwalks and billboards all over the world, and yet revealing her vulnerability to Lincoln was the scariest, most terrifying thing of all.

'Probably not.' She wrapped her arms around her body against the chill of the night air.

There was a lengthy silence.

Lincoln stepped closer and lifted her chin with two of his fingers, meshing his gaze with hers. 'It wasn't my best moment, having that photo circulated of me with that young woman.' He gave a rueful twist of his mouth, then lowered his hand from her face and continued, 'You should have heard the dressing-down Sylvia gave me. She thought it was unspeakably crass. But I was angry and bitter. It's not often I get blindsided by someone—especially someone who'd claimed they loved me.'

But I did love you.

The words were stuck behind the wall of her pride. The pride she needed to keep from getting hurt all over again.

Elodie moved further away from him, wrapping her arms around her middle to ward off the sudden chill of the night air. 'Look—I was young, and I had stars in my eyes. You showed me a world I'd never had access to before. A world of wealth and privilege and private jets and God knows what else. I fooled myself into thinking you cared about me, but what you cared about was having a beautiful wife. I'd have completed your successful lifestyle. A good-looking wife who you saw as an asset rather than a person in her own right. But you didn't offer me your heart in return.'

'I seem to remember you made the most of our breakup.'

The mocking tone was back, even more biting than before. And the steely look in his eyes was harder than the diamonds on her finger.

Elodie went back into the trench of her pride. 'And why shouldn't I have made the most of it? The sponsors approached me—not me them. I did realise it gave me the perfect opportunity to lift my profile, and I didn't see any reason I shouldn't use it. I was only doing itty-bitty modelling jobs before that, most of which only paid a pittance, and I found them demeaning. I wanted to get more control over the photos and the labels I wore, so shoot me for using our breakup to do it. Besides, you're the one who always says you shouldn't let emotions get in the way of a good business decision. I was simply taking your advice.'

There was a ringing silence.

Then Lincoln's mouth began to twitch with a smile. 'Methinks I've been hoist by my own petard.'

Elodie mock-pouted at him. 'That'll teach you for having one rule for you and another one for everyone else.'

He stepped towards her again and took her by the upper arms. His eyes meshed with hers, and there was a lopsided smile on his lips. He lifted his hand to her face and stroked his finger down the slope of her nose. 'That's another thing I missed about you. You always stood up to me.'

'What? No one else has since?'

He gave a rueful movement of his lips. 'Not quite like you do.' He stroked her bottom lip with his thumb. 'I'm surrounded by sycophants most of the time—people intent on pleasing me. It gets boring after a while.'

Elodie placed her hands against his chest, felt his warmth seeping into her like the rays of the sun. Her lower body brushed against his and a wave of longing swept through her. 'I'm glad you didn't find me boring. But if you were missing a good old ding-dong fight, why didn't you just call me? I'm sure we could have found something to argue about.'

She was only half joking. She had missed their fights too. In fact, she had missed way more than that. She had missed everything about him.

His eyes drifted to her mouth. 'That night we ran in to each other in Soho...' He grimaced, as if the memory pained him. 'When I saw you go off with Fraser MacDiarmid I was shocked at how much I wanted to stop you.'

Elodie arched her eyebrows. 'You said you weren't jealous that night.'

His expression had a hint of sheepishness about it. 'Seeing you again was...difficult. I'd seen you heaps of time on billboards or in magazine spreads and on television, but not in the flesh.' His eyes came back to hers, dark and glittering. 'I was jealous, angry... disappointed that it wasn't me you were going off with instead of him. The thing is, I'd never felt jealous before. It annoyed me that I felt it then.'

Elodie wasn't fool enough to think his jealousy signalled love. He was a proud man who had been publicly humiliated by her jilting him. Seeing her with another man would have triggered him in the same way she had been triggered by seeing him with his beautiful and clearly devoted new partner that night.

She lifted her hands to the tops of his broad shoulders, then slid them down his muscled arms to his strong wrists. His fingers entwined with hers and heat coursed through her body. 'We're going to have to deal with the chance of running into each other in the future—I mean, once we divorce.'

It seemed a good a time as any to remind him of the time frame on their marriage. To remind herself.

Lincoln placed one of his hands in the small of her back, bringing her up against him. 'Let's not mention the *D* word until after Nina passes.'

'But what if she doesn't die within our time frame? I mean, it can happen, you know… People go into remission, or a new drug is released, or—'

'Our agreement is six months and six months only.'

The edge of intractability in his tone was just the reminder she needed to keep her emotions in check.

'Fine.' She pulled out of his hold and sent a careless hand through her hair. 'I'm going back to bed.'

She turned and walked through the French doors, back into the bedroom, aware of Lincoln's footsteps following her. He came up behind her and placed his hands on her hips, pulling her against him. His hands cupped her breasts and a shiver of anticipation coursed over her flesh.

'Want me to join you?'

He spoke against the sensitive skin of her neck, sending another hot shiver racing down her spine like a cartwheeling fiery coal.

'I thought you didn't like spending the whole night with your casual lovers any more?'

Lincoln turned her so she was facing him. His smile was sardonic, his eyes glittering. 'You're not a casual lover—you're my wife.'

'For six months and six months only.' Elodie followed up her statement with a sugar-sweet smile. 'That's still a lot of nights sharing a bed.'

His hands skimmed down the sides of her body, from her shoulders, past her ribcage and waist, to settle on her hips, his gaze smouldering. 'Then let's not waste a single one of them.'

And his mouth came down and sealed hers hotly, explosively, possessively.

It was an urgent kiss that sent a river of fire through her blood and her body. Her inner core turned to molten lava within seconds, her need of him so intense it surged in pulsing and pounding waves through her most intimate flesh.

Lincoln tumbled with her to the bed, only stopping long enough to apply a condom. He rolled her over so she straddled him, his hands caressing her breasts with thrilling expertise. He guided himself into her, his expression a grimace of pleasure at the contact of aroused male flesh against aroused female flesh.

'You feel so damn good...' he groaned.

'You took the words right out of my mouth.'

Not to mention taking her breath away.

Elodie moved with him, the rocking motion of their bodies sending her over the edge within moments. She gasped out loud, riding out the powerful orgasm, her hair swishing wildly about her shoulders, her body so rattled and shaken by ripples of pleasure it was like being transported to another world. A world of intense sensuality where no thoughts were necessary.

This was not the time to think of the temporary nature of their relationship. This was not the time to think about the love she had for him that put her at so much risk of heartbreak. This was the time to enjoy a moment of pure ecstatic bliss, of two perfectly in tune bodies.

Elodie came floating back down from the stratosphere to watch Lincoln shuddering through his own release. It looked and sounded as mind-blowing as her own. She scooped her hair back over one of her shoulders and smiled down at him. 'You look like you had a good time.'

He gave a deep sigh. 'The best.'

Elodie lay over him with her head on his chest, their bodies still intimately joined. His hands stroked the curves of her bottom in lazy strokes that sent goosebumps popping up all over her skin.

'If you don't stop doing that, you're going to have to make love to me all over again.'

'Maybe that's exactly what I want to do.'

'So soon?'

'You bet.'

He flipped her so she was lying on her back, then swiftly disposed of the used condom before replacing it with a fresh one. He came back to her, leaning his weight on one elbow, one of his strongly muscled legs flung over one of hers. His other hand caressed her thigh in long slow movements that sent tingles down to her curling toes.

'I could make love to you all night.'

CHAPTER NINE

THE NEXT COUPLE of days passed in a blur of activity. Spending time with Nina was clearly a priority for Lincoln, which only made Elodie love and respect him more, but he also managed to show Elodie some of the tourist spots in the town—including the Roman theatre and the fortress castle.

They walked hand in hand as they explored the sights, and she tried to pretend they were just like any loved-up couple on their honeymoon. There were even times when she caught Lincoln looking at her with an indulgent look on his face, making her wonder if some of his bitterness about their breakup was finally melting away.

Certainly, there was no trace of it in his lovemaking. The passion they shared never ceased to amaze her. It seemed to be getting more intense, and there were moments of tenderness too, that were particularly poignant given their marriage was only temporary.

It was poignant too, to see Lincoln's relationship with his biological mother growing each day.

It touched Elodie to see the care he had for her, the way he made sure she had everything she needed. The villa and its grounds were immaculate, and managed with expertise, and the staff were friendly and supportive.

Elodie couldn't help comparing the lovely Alita with Morag. How could there be two such different housekeepers? One was so helpful, the other so spiteful. One made her feel welcome, the other made her feel like trailer trash, triggering the emotions of the past, when others had done the same. It made the thought of going back to London daunting—not to mention the prospect of leaving Nina, and wondering if it would be the last time they'd see her.

The morning of their departure, Nina wrapped her arms around Elodie in a warm, motherly hug. 'Take care of yourself, my dear. Don't work too hard, will you? And promise to come and see me again soon, yes?'

Elodie blinked back tears, her heart suddenly feeling cramped inside her chest cavity. 'I promise. Thank you for making me feel so welcome.' She eased back to look at the older woman, who was also tearing up. 'I'm so glad you and Lincoln found each other at last.'

Nina's smile was happy-sad. 'I waited a long time to make contact. Too long. But I wasn't sure if he would want to meet me. After all, I gave him up as a week-old baby. Some adoptees find that very hard to understand—why their birth mother gave them away. But I always loved him. I only ever wanted the best for him.'

Elodie stood back as Lincoln hugged Nina and said his own goodbyes. He had better control over his emotions, but she sensed he was also well aware that this could be the last time he saw Nina. She saw it in the set of his jaw, the fixed smile, the shadowed eyes, the aura of sadness that enveloped him.

Once they were in the car, with Elonzo driving, on their way to the airport, Elodie placed her hand on Lincoln's thigh. 'I really like Nina. She's so warm and friendly.'

He took her hand and gave it a gentle squeeze. 'Yeah, she's great.' His voice was sandpaper-rough. 'I'm glad she liked you.'

Elodie glanced at her wedding and engagement rings, glittering on her hand. 'Yes, well…it would've been a disaster if she hadn't, given you've gone to the trouble of marrying me and all.'

His gaze met hers, his expression inscrutable. 'Has it been such a trial so far?'

She leaned closer to plant a kiss on his lips. 'No…' Her voice came out a little husky. 'But I can't say I'm looking forward to living in the same house as Mean Morag. Alita is so lovely and sweet. She falls over herself to help.'

'I hope you don't call Morag that to her face?'

'No, of course not.'

He sighed and ruffled the loose strands of her hair. 'I'll have a word with her about reducing her hours. That way you won't have to run into her so often.'

'I probably won't be home during the day much anyway. I have work to do. I've got to find a studio—

preferably close to the centre of London, which will cost a bomb, but—'

'I know of a place you could use,' Lincoln said. 'It's around the corner from my office—the one that's currently being renovated. It has space for a showroom as well.'

A flicker of excitement coursed through her blood. 'Really? How much will the rent be, do you think?'

'I'll have a word with the landlord. He might do mates' rates or something.'

'Wow, that would be awesome.'

He brought her hand up to his chest, his eyes meshing with hers. 'You might not believe this, but I really want you to succeed.'

Elodie didn't ask for clarification, because she already knew what was behind his motivation for her success. Her career would be all she was left with after their marriage came to an end. It would be her consolation prize.

'I'll do my best,' she said.

Within a few of days of coming back to London, Elodie was setting up her studio with Elspeth's help. Some of the furniture had yet to arrive, and there was a lot more to do in terms of preparing her creative space, but it was like a dream come true to have her own place at last.

'I've got a good feeling about this venture of yours,' Elspeth said, unloading some fabric swatches from a box. 'I can't wait to come in and have some fancy evening wear designed for me by you.'

'Hey, I thought you didn't like dressing up?' Elodie teased. 'What happened to the shy librarian archivist who only wore brown and beige and flat shoes?'

Elspeth pulled the plastic wrapping off one of the velvet showroom chairs and gave a dreamy smile. 'I've decided it's much more fun being a butterfly than a moth.' She bundled the wrapping into a ball and added, 'You haven't told me much about your trip to Spain apart from how nice Nina was. How was it?'

'It was good.'

'Only "good"?'

Elodie took the ball of plastic from her twin and stuffed it in the box she had set aside for recycling. 'We're not having a paper marriage any more.'

Elspeth's eyes twinkled. 'Wow!'

'Wow, indeed.' Elodie picked up one of the sketching sets she'd ordered and placed it on the table. 'This is probably way too much information to share, even for a twin sister, but I've never really enjoyed making love with anyone other than Lincoln.' She glanced at her twin. 'Is that weird, or what?'

'It's not weird at all,' Elspeth said. 'It shows you care about him. You do, don't you?'

Elodie sighed. 'Way more than I should, given we're only staying married for a matter of months.'

'That might change. I mean, Lincoln might change his mind and offer you more.'

'He was pretty blunt about it. Six months and six months only.'

'But he changed his mind about the paper marriage, right?'

Elodie picked up another parcel from the box she was unloading, a small frown tugging at her brow. 'I haven't decided yet if he always intended to tweak the rules or if I managed to convince him. He's so hard to read sometimes.'

Elspeth started to unwrap another velvet chair, a small smile playing about her mouth. 'I can only imagine the lengths you went to in order to change his mind.'

Elodie laughed. 'Now, that *would* be sharing way too much information.'

Elodie got back to Lincoln's London home to find Morag preparing dinner in the kitchen. She hadn't seen much of the housekeeper since she and Lincoln had returned from Spain. She had deliberately stayed away during Morag's working hours. But now that she had no choice but to interact with her, Elodie decided to try a new tactic—to act her way into feeling more positive about the grumpy housekeeper.

It was worth a try. Anything was worth a try.

'Can I do anything to help?'

Morag wiped the back of her hand across her forehead. 'No. I can manage.'

Elodie narrowed her gaze on the older woman's strange-looking pallor. She had a greyish tinge to her skin and beads of perspiration peppered her forehead. 'Are you okay?'

Morag gripped the edge of the kitchen bench with her hands. 'I… I think I might need some insulin…

I might have missed a dose…or eaten the wrong thing…'

Elodie rushed over and took her by the shoulders. 'Let me help you. Come and sit down and I'll get your insulin for you. Where is it?'

Morag sank into the chair with a sigh of relief. 'In my bedroom…' She took a gasping breath and slumped forward with her head bent over her knees. 'In the chest of drawers…top drawer, I think.'

'I'm going to call an ambulance.'

'Don't you dare. I'll be fine once I've had a dose.'

'Maybe you should lie down while I get it?' Elodie suggested. 'I don't want you to fall off that chair.'

Morag lifted her head to glare at her. 'Just bring me the insulin, will you?'

Elodie ground her teeth and ran upstairs to the top floor, where Morag had a small suite of rooms for when she stayed over. She rushed over to the chest of drawers, but the insulin wasn't in the top drawer as Morag had thought. She opened the second and third drawers, rustling through the housekeeper's belongings, but failed to find any medication.

The fourth and bottom drawer was stiff to open, and while she doubted the medication would be stored there, she thought it best to check anyway. She finally managed to get the drawer open and rummaged around the contents. Her eyes suddenly homed in on a velvet ring box, and her heart came to a complete standstill. She stared at the box for countless seconds, her heartbeat restarting with a loud *ba-boom*, *ba-boom, ba-boom* that made her suspect she was having her own medical crisis.

She reached for the box with a hand that wasn't quite steady, opening it to find her old engagement ring glittering there in all its brilliance. Something dropped like a tombstone in her stomach. Morag had the ring. All this time, the housekeeper had had the ring. But why?

Elodie heard the sound of Lincoln's firm footsteps coming along the corridor and quickly stashed the ring back in the drawer. She tried to shove it closed. The drawer wouldn't close all the way, but there wasn't time to worry about that. She straightened and glanced around the room, and saw an insulin kit sitting on a chair next to the bed. She snatched it up just as Lincoln came through the door.

'You found it? Great.' He took it off her and raced back downstairs, with Elodie in hot pursuit. 'I called an ambulance. It should be here any second now.'

'I offered to, but Morag insisted I didn't.'

'She can be difficult about her illness. She hasn't really accepted it.'

They got back to the kitchen and Lincoln helped administer a dose of insulin as if he had been moonlighting as a physician for years. Morag recovered within a few minutes, but by then the ambulance had arrived and Lincoln insisted she go to hospital to be checked out.

'But what about dinner?' Morag said.

'I'll sort it out,' Elodie said. 'You just concentrate on getting well again.'

Within a short time the paramedics had taken Morag away and Elodie and Lincoln were left alone.

Lincoln took Elodie by the hands, his expression rich with concern. 'Are you okay? You look like you're in shock.'

Elodie *was* in shock. Deep shock. Her heart was still pounding, sweat was trickling down between her shoulder blades, and her stomach was churning along with her brain. Here was her chance to tell him about the ring she had found, but for some reason she couldn't bring herself to do it. What if he thought she herself had planted it there? What if he didn't believe she had found it while looking for the insulin kit?

But if he did believe her, she realised it would poison his relationship with his housekeeper. The breach of trust would be hard to forgive—especially when Morag had worked for him for so long. Besides, she wanted to hear Morag's explanation first.

'I—I'm fine…' She forced a smile that didn't quite work. 'I'm not good in a crisis. Just ask Elspeth. Sick people terrify me.'

Lincoln stroked her hair away from her face, his gaze steady on hers. 'You did a great job of taking care of Morag.'

She gave a dismissive snort, her eyes drifting away from his. 'So, how was your day?'

He reached up to loosen his tie. 'Not bad. How did you go at the studio?'

'It was great. Elspeth came to help me unpack the stuff that's arrived so far. There's still heaps to do, but it feels so good to have my own space. I can't thank you enough for organising it for me.'

He gave her chin a playful brush with his fingers. 'It's my pleasure.'

Elodie plastered another smile on her lips and turned for the kitchen, saying over her shoulder, 'Give me half an hour or so and I'll have dinner ready for you.'

'You're starting to sound very wifey.'

There was a note of amusement in his tone.

She turned around to smile back at him. 'Make the most of it, baby. It's only for six months, remember?'

And then she disappeared into the kitchen.

Lincoln tugged his silk tie the rest of the way out of his collar, threading it through his fingers, a frown pulling at his forehead. Elodie was always reminding him of the temporary nature of their relationship. Was that for her benefit or his? He knew the time frame well enough—he was the one who'd put it in place. And it needed to stay in place, in spite of how well they were getting on.

Settling down to domesticity with Elodie was out of the question. Firstly, because he didn't want to lay himself open to the sort of heartache his father had gone through after losing his mother—loving for a lifetime contained certain devastation, for one partner always outlived the other. It was a fact of life and one he wanted to avoid experiencing first-hand. And secondly, because Elodie was like him—career-focussed.

She had left him before because she had wanted a career more than she wanted to be with him.

Now he was doing all he could to facilitate her career—it was the least he could do to repay her for how warmly she had bonded with Nina. He had hoped they would connect, but he hadn't dared hope they would get on as well as they had. It made him feel a little less compromised about the game of charades he and Elodie were playing.

But there were times when it didn't feel like a charade.

It felt real...scarily real.

Elodie was still mulling over the engagement ring hidden in the drawer upstairs when Lincoln came into the kitchen.

She quickly hung a tea towel over the oven door. 'No peeking. I want to surprise you with dinner.'

'It smells delicious.'

'It needs a few more minutes. Do you want a glass of wine?'

'Sure. You want one?'

'Not tonight.'

The last thing she wanted was to loosen her tongue with wine. The engagement ring incident was still playing on her mind. She couldn't work out why Morag would have done such a thing. Why hadn't she sold the ring? Why had she kept it after all this time? What could the housekeeper hope to achieve by keeping it stashed away? It didn't make any sense.

'I'm having an AFD.'

'Pardon?'

'An alcohol-free day.'

'Right...'

'But you go ahead.'

Lincoln took a bottle of orange juice out of the integrated fridge. 'I'm fine with juice. Would you prefer mineral water?'

'That would be perfect.'

A short time later they were seated in the dining room. Elodie served the chicken chasseur she'd made, along with steamed beans and a potato dish with onions and a dash of cream and fresh herbs.

She picked up her glass of mineral water. *'Bon appetit.'*

Lincoln smiled and picked up his glass, clinked it against hers. 'So, when did you develop an interest in cooking? I seem to recall you could barely scramble an egg when we were together.'

She put her glass down and picked up her cutlery, sending him a glance across the candlelit table. 'Life living out of hotels can be pretty boring. The food starts to taste all the same. I made a point of using my time at home between photo shoots as a chance to experiment. I did a cooking class in Italy, and then another one in France. They were heaps of fun.'

'I'm impressed.'

Elodie shrugged off his compliment. 'It's not that hard. But I freak out a bit when I cook for Elspeth.'

'Because of her allergy?'

'Yeah.' She shuddered and continued, 'Seeing Morag collapse like that was a bit triggering, to be honest. What if neither of us had been home? What if she'd lost consciousness and we'd found her on the floor, and it was too late, and—'

'Elodie, sweetheart.' His voice cut across her panicked speech with calm authority. 'It didn't happen, okay? She's safe and sound in hospital and she will be back to work tomorrow, if I'm any judge.'

Elodie put her cutlery down, her appetite completely deserting her. 'Sorry.' She flashed him an effigy of a smile. 'It's been a long day. I think I'll just clear away and go to bed.'

She put her napkin to one side and began to push her chair back. Lincoln rose from his own chair and came around to help her. He took her in his arms and gathered her close, resting his chin on the top of her head.

'Seven years ago you never really told me much about what it was like for you, growing up with Elspeth and her allergy. You've told me more in the last few days than you did the whole time we were together.'

Elodie laid her cheek against his chest, enjoying the warmth and protectiveness of his embrace and the deep reverberation of his voice beneath her ear. 'I guess we talked about other stuff or didn't talk at all. Or at least not about stuff that was deep and serious.'

He lifted her chin from his chest and meshed his gaze with hers. 'I should have told you about my adoption. I have a habit of compartmentalising my life. I'm not sure it's a healthy or wise thing to do.'

She slipped her arms around his waist. 'At least

you're aware of doing it. That's half the battle, surely? Awareness.'

'It sure is.' He placed his hands on her hips, his expression warm and tender. 'I'll clear this away while you go upstairs and get ready for bed. I'll be up soon.'

'But I'm such a messy cook. There's stuff everywhere in the kitchen.'

'You're not the only one who's become a little more domesticated in the last few years. Now, off you go. I won't take no for an answer.'

Elodie would have put up more of a fight, but she suddenly realised how completely exhausted she was. Her emotions were in a whirlpool and she didn't know how to process them. She was used to blocking out things she didn't want to think about. Used to pushing thoughts to the back of her mind and leaving them there, like stuffing old clothes she didn't want to wear again to the back of the wardrobe.

But the engagement ring sitting in that drawer in Morag's room was playing on her mind so much it made it hard to think about anything else.

Should she tell Lincoln, or leave things until she could talk to Morag? How could she tell Lincoln and be sure he would believe her?

Sure, they were talking and communicating in a way they hadn't done in the past, but it didn't guarantee he would trust her version of events. She had been the one to publicly humiliate him by jilting him. It would be reasonable for him to assume she had sold the ring to finance her career. If she produced it now, it would be her word against his long-term housekeeper's. And he had never trusted her word against Morag's in the past.

It had always been difficult for her to put her trust in someone, to believe they'd have her back no matter what. That they'd *believe* her. She had been portrayed in the press as scatty and fickle—a wild party girl who couldn't care less what people thought of her.

But she did care.

Was it foolish to hope Lincoln might finally trust her now?

Lincoln worked at restoring order to the kitchen for the next forty minutes. Elodie hadn't been wrong when she'd called herself a messy cook—it looked as if she had used every pot and utensil. He was used to good food—his housekeeper was an excellent cook, who always prepared nutritious and interesting meals. But seeing the effort Elodie had gone to over dinner— especially after experiencing the shock of Morag's medical episode—deeply impressed him.

He was learning more and more about her upbringing, and he realised now how little he had understood her in the past. No wonder she had looked done in and gone to bed early. She had been triggered by his housekeeper's sudden collapse—no doubt because of all the times she had witnessed her twin suffering an attack of anaphylaxis.

What could be more terrifying to a small child than to see her twin sister desperately ill? He hadn't realised how pushed aside she had felt by her mother's overprotectiveness of Elspeth. Of course any parent would struggle to balance the needs of their children under such difficult circumstances. But Elodie had hinted at the way she had fought to be noticed—by seeking attention by negative means. Hadn't she done that during their previous relationship? Hadn't her constant bickering over inconsequential things been a continuation of that pattern of behaviour?

Lincoln finally made it upstairs, only to find Elodie soundly asleep. She was curled up in a ball like a sleeping kitten, her hair a red-gold cloud splayed across the pillow. He pulled the covers up a little more and then leaned down to press a light-as-air kiss to the top of her head. She made a soft murmur and burrowed deeper into the mattress, her eyes remaining closed, her dark lashes like miniature fans resting softly against her cheeks.

He stood looking at her for a long moment, and felt something in his chest tightening, straining, like a silk thread pulling against his heart. This subtle shift in their relationship was bringing up other issues he wasn't sure he wanted to face.

But the timeline was set.

He had insisted it was non-negotiable.

Damn it, it *was* non-negotiable.

And yet something about being with Elodie now made it harder for him to imagine going back to his playboy lifestyle. Or was it because he didn't like thinking about her with someone else? He hadn't considered himself the green-eyed monster type, but thinking about her with someone else tied his gut into knots. Strangely, he had found himself confessing to her how eaten with jealousy he had been that night they'd run into each other in Soho—even though he had rigorously denied it before.

Showing any hint of vulnerability was normally anathema to him. He didn't do it in his professional life. He didn't do it in his personal life.

He didn't do it, period.

So why was he even tempted to do it now?

CHAPTER TEN

ELODIE SIGHED AND rolled over in bed, opening her eyes to find Lincoln lying on his side, watching her in the moonlight. She ran a lazy hand over the dark stubble on his jaw. 'You really are a dreadful insomniac these days, aren't you?'

He gave a crooked smile that made something slip sideways in her stomach.

'I like watching you sleep.'

She wriggled closer, her legs tangling with his beneath the bedcovers. 'I'm not asleep now.'

'So I see.'

Her hand drifted down to the proud rise of his erection. 'What are you thinking about?' she asked.

'Right now?' His tone was so dry it almost crackled, his eyes glittering darkly.

'Right now.'

'I'm a little cognitively impaired right at this very moment, with you touching me like that.'

'Like this?' Elodie ran her hand up and down the length of his shaft, her own arousal intensified by feeling the insistent throb of his.

He groaned and pulled her hand away, moving over her so she was beneath the weight of his body. He caged her in with his arms, his gaze holding hers in an erotic lock that sent tingles to her core. 'I want you.'

The raw urgency in his voice matched the desire pounding through her body. 'I want you too—just in case you hadn't picked up on that vibe.'

'You're not exactly subtle.'

She gave him a twinkling smile. 'Do you want me to be?'

'God, no. I love it when you're so forthright. It turns me on.'

He lowered his mouth to hers in a spine-tingling kiss that lifted each and every hair on her head. His tongue tangled with hers, darting and diving and duelling in a cat-and-mouse caper that thrilled her senses.

He lifted his mouth off hers to work his way down her body, leaving a hot pathway of kisses along her naked skin. He caressed her breasts with his lips and his tongue, sending waves of pleasure through her as strong as electrical pulses. He worked his way down her stomach, circling her belly button with the teasing touch of his tongue. She sucked in a breath as he went lower, his lips exploring her most intimate flesh of all.

She arched her back like a sinuous cat, giving herself up to the sensual attention of his mouth. He knew her body so well, so intimately, there was no question of her not responding. She did—powerfully, passionately, volubly. Her panting cries were almost primal, the thrashing of her body equally so. Her orgasm went on and on, carrying her along on a rushing tide that was almost frightening in its intensity.

She finally collapsed back against the pillows. 'Oh, God, I can't believe you did that. I thought it was never going to end.'

Lincoln gave her a smouldering look and leaned across her to access a condom. He slipped it on and came back to her, one of his hands brushing her wildly disordered hair off her face. 'I love watching you come.'

Elodie scrunched up her face self-consciously. 'Eek! I can only imagine how ugly I look.'

'You couldn't look ugly if you tried.'

She traced the strong line of his collarbone with her finger, her gaze lowered from his. 'Beauty isn't everything…and it fades eventually.' She raised her eyes back to his. 'Millions of people have seen me in sexy lingerie and swimwear, but I don't think they actually see *me*…the real me…mostly because I haven't wanted them to.'

'But now?'

She chewed one side of her mouth. 'I've played on my looks for as long as I can remember. I've used them to get where I wanted to go. Unlike Elspeth, who tried not to be noticed at all. But I want more now. I want to be noticed for my skills as a designer—not because I rock a skimpy bikini.'

'I'm going to miss seeing you in those skimpy bikinis.'

She angled her head at him. 'So you've been checking out some billboards and magazine spreads, have you? I noticed one in your office. Did you know I was in it or was that just a lucky purchase?'

'Lucky purchase.' His eyes shone like wet paint. 'Although coming across you on a billboard almost caused me to run off the road a couple of times.'

'No doubt because you were furious with me for having the audacity to use our breakup as a platform for my success.'

There was a small silence.

'I was angry…livid, actually…' His voice trailed away as if something had changed in his attitude towards her since then.

'But not now?'

He brushed another strand of hair off her face, tucking it gently behind her ear. 'It's hard to be angry with you when you're lying naked in my bed.'

Elodie stroked her hand down his flat abdomen, her smile teasing. 'Do you want me to get dressed?'

His gaze glinted and he lowered his mouth to just above hers. 'Not yet.'

Elodie linked her arms around his neck, the thrill of his lips and tongue against hers sending her pulse racing off the charts all over again. He entered her body with a deep thrust that sent shockwave after shockwave of pleasure through her. His movements were slow at first, but he gradually increased his pace, driving her closer and closer to the point of no return.

The tension built in her body—the delicious tension that incorporated each and every piece of intricate tissue and muscle in her feminine flesh. She arched her pelvis to seek more friction, wanting more, needing more, aching for more. He slipped his hand between their bodies and caressed her swollen flesh, sending her over the edge within seconds. The orgasm rippled through her in smashing, crashing, tumbling waves, sending her senses into a whirlpool of earth-shattering ecstasy.

Lincoln followed her with his own release, the vigorous pumping action of his body sending another wave of tumultuous pleasure through her slick and swollen flesh. He gave a guttural groan and pitched forward over her, giving a whole-body shudder as he spilled his essence.

It was not often Elodie was rendered speechless, but her body was so acutely aware of every part of his where it touched her. The aftershocks were still rumbling through every inch of her flesh, and her heart was hammering against his chest where it was pressed against hers. The physical bliss was unlike any she had experienced with anyone else. And she knew without a doubt that even if she went on to have dozens of subsequent partners no one would ever be able to draw from her such a mind-blowing response.

The realisation of what lay ahead of her once their six months were up—the aching loneliness, the emptiness of shallow going-nowhere relationships—almost made her cry. Almost.

She bit down on her lower lip and squeezed her eyes closed over the sting of tears. She had no right to be upset. She had agreed to the terms and was already enjoying the benefit of them. Her bank account was full of money. More money than she had ever dreamed to see there. Luxury fabrics were on order, due to arrive this week. The studio was just about up and running. She had dozens of sketches in her workbooks and on her laptop. She had staff interviews set up in the coming days. Promotional work to see to… interviews and planning meetings. She even had clients waiting for her to design for them—not just Elspeth and Nina, but other friends and acquaintances.

Her dream was finally coming to fruition and she wanted to cry? She had to get a grip on herself. Emotions and business didn't mix, right? That was Lincoln's mantra and it had to be hers.

It *had* to be. Otherwise she would get her heart smashed to pieces.

Lincoln rolled her over so she was lying face to face with him on her side. He propped himself up on one elbow and stroked his other hand down the slope of her cheek, his frowning eyes searching hers. 'What's wrong?'

She forced her lips into a tight smile and rolled away, sitting upright and tossing her hair back over one shoulder. 'Don't mind me. I'm just trying to recover from having multiple orgasms for the first time in seven years.'

He sat up and shuffled over so he was sitting beside her on the bed. One of his hands stroked down the length of her spine—a warm, soothing stroke that loosened each and every vertebra.

'If it's any comfort, I'm a little shell-shocked too.'

He bent his head and planted a soft kiss to the

top of her shoulder, the touch of his lips making her skin tingle.

'More than a little, actually.'

Elodie turned her head to meet his blue-green gaze. She lifted her hand to his face and traced the prominent line of each of his eyebrows. 'That's good. I'd hate to be the only one feeling dazzled.'

He slid his hand under the curtain of her hair and brought his mouth down to just above hers. 'That's what you do best, sweetheart. Dazzle.'

And he closed the distance between their mouths with a blistering kiss.

It was almost two weeks later when Morag returned to work. Elodie was due home first, as Lincoln was flying back from a meeting in Dublin later that night. He'd asked her to go with him and stay a couple of extra days, but she'd declined, citing another staff interview as well as working on her designs for Nina and helping Elspeth prepare for her wedding.

She was determined to keep her career her main focus. Dropping everything to follow Lincoln around the globe was not going to build her career to the level she desired. If he'd been disappointed with her declining his invitation, he hadn't shown it. But then, why would he? He wasn't in love with her. The arrangement he had with her was temporary. Once their marriage was over he would move on with his playboy lifestyle as if nothing had changed.

Morag was already ensconced in the kitchen, an apron tied around her waist and a wooden spoon in her hand. 'Lincoln told me to take a few more days off but I wanted to get back to work.' She stirred the mixture in the bowl in front of her and added gruffly, 'Thanks for helping me the other night.'

'I was worried about you. Are you feeling better now?'

'I'm fine. I just have to adjust my diet a bit.' Morag gave her a sheepish glance and added, 'No more cookies and chocolate.'

Elodie pulled out one of the bar stools next to the kitchen island and perched on it, wrapping her ankles around the legs. 'Gosh, I can't remember the last time I had a cookie or chocolate.'

Morag frowned. 'Is that because you're always dieting…because of modelling and all?'

'No, not really. It's because I never had them growing up. It was too risky having them in the house because of my twin's nut allergy.'

Morag met her gaze across the width of the bench. 'There's something I want to talk to you about…'

The hesitancy in the older woman's tone was unusual, not to mention her expression. Normally so brisk and forthright, and always wearing a frown, this time she had a worried look on her face.

'When you were looking for my insulin…' She swallowed convulsively and continued, 'I noticed the bottom drawer wasn't closed properly…that things were shifted around in there…'

'Why did you keep it?' Elodie decided to get straight to the point.

The older woman's cheeks developed a dull flush

along her cheekbones. 'I tried to tell Lincoln I'd found it on the hall table, but he was so hungover after the wedding day and so angry…he wouldn't have your name mentioned. I was shocked when I saw it there. I didn't think you'd return it.'

'Because you had me pegged as a gold-digger?'

Morag's blush deepened. 'I know I should have tried to tell him a bit later, but I thought it best not to.'

'Why?'

'I thought if I told him you'd returned it he might consider asking you to come back to him.'

'But you didn't want him to do that, did you?'

Morag pressed her lips together and let go of the handle of the wooden spoon. 'I didn't think you loved him the way he deserved to be loved.' She swallowed again and met Elodie's gaze with an imploring one. 'Please don't tell him what I did. I can't lose this job. It's the only thing I have that brings me pleasure, a sense of purpose, a sense of being needed… I can't tell you how much *he* means to me. My own children don't speak to me now, because their father poisoned them against me. Lincoln is like a son to me. I know that sounds ridiculous, and sentimental, but I watched him grow up. Me and Rosemary, his adoptive mother, were at school together. He's the only connection I have with her now. I don't know his brother and sister the way I know him. I've known him all his life and I can't bear for him to think badly of me.'

Elodie jumped down from the stool and raked a hand through her hair. 'I'm sorry you've had such awful stuff happen to you. No woman deserves to be treated like that. And to lose contact with your children…well, that's heart-wrenching. But you're asking a lot of me to say nothing to Lincoln about this.'

'I know, and I won't really blame you if you choose to tell him. I haven't exactly been very welcoming to you.'

Elodie gave a long-winded sigh. 'I'm not going to tell him. Besides, he probably wouldn't believe me if I did.'

There was a pulsing silence.

'You do love him, don't you?' Morag's expression was tortured with lines of guilt. 'You've always loved him…' Her words trailed off in an agony of realisation.

Elodie stretched her lips into a humourless smile. 'More fool me. He doesn't love me back.'

'I know how that feels…loving someone who doesn't love you the way you love them. You live in hope, wasting years of your life, and for what? To be rejected, cast aside. But you have a second chance with Lincoln. He's married you, after all, and—'

'Our marriage is a sham. We're only together to please his dying biological mother—Nina. But I think you already suspected that.'

'But you're sleeping together?'

Elodie gave her a worldly look. 'It's what you might call a marriage of convenience with benefits.'

Morag opened and closed her mouth, seemingly speechless for a moment. 'I wish I could undo the past. If I had my time over I would tell Lincoln about the ring whether he wanted to listen or not.' Tears shone in her eyes and she continued in a harrowed tone, 'I know it's too much to ask you to forgive me...'

Elodie walked around to Morag's side of the bench and wrapped her arms around her in a hug. 'It's in the past...let's leave it there.'

How could she insist on the older woman revealing her role in the disappearing engagement ring? As much as she wanted Lincoln to know the truth, another part of her understood the motivation behind Morag's seven-year silence. After all, Elodie had her own secret—she loved Lincoln and always had.

And there was no point revealing it now.

Lincoln came home a couple of days later and immediately noticed a different atmosphere in the house. His housekeeper and Elodie seemed to have resolved their differences, for he found them cooking together in the kitchen. Elodie had a streak of flour on one cheek and her hands were busily kneading what looked like pizza dough. Morag was tearing leaves of fresh basil off a plant near the sink, and chatting to Elodie about a trip to Italy she had taken some years ago.

'Oh, hi, Lincoln.'

Elodie looked up with a smile that was so welcoming and bright something in his chest pinged.

'How was your Dublin trip?'

'Fine.' He stepped further into the room. 'Looks like you two are busy.'

'Elodie's teaching me how to make pizza from

scratch,' Morag said. 'I've only ever used shop-bought bases. This is so much better.'

'Smells good so far.' Lincoln dropped a kiss to Elodie's lips, then dusted the flour off her face. 'How's the studio going?'

'Great,' Elodie said. 'I've employed two assistants and they're helping me organise things for my first show. It'll take a few months to get ready, but I'm hoping to have a collection together for spring next year.'

'I'll take over now, if you like,' Morag said. 'You two go and have a pre-dinner drink in the sitting room and I'll let you know when dinner's ready.'

'Thanks, Morag, you're a gem,' Lincoln said.

A minute or two later, Lincoln handed Elodie a glass of champagne in the sitting room. 'Here you go.'

'Lovely, thanks.' She smiled and took a sip, and then screwed up her nose and frowned.

'Is something wrong?'

She put the glass down on a nearby side table. 'I can't believe I'm saying this, but I seem to have lost my taste for champagne. I might just have a juice or mineral water instead.'

Lincoln got the juice for her and then sat beside on her the sofa, his body angled so he could look at her. She was dressed in casual clothes—a pair of black leggings and a grey sweater that had slid off one of her slim shoulders. Her hair was tied in a makeshift bun on top of her head and her face was free of makeup. He could have sat staring at her for hours.

'You seem to have affected a truce with Morag,' he said, to break the silence.

Elodie's gaze drifted away from his to look at her glass of juice. 'Yes, well…we've come to an understanding.'

'You looked very chummy out there. What brought about the change?'

She tucked one of her legs under her and brushed away a stray hair from her face. 'She thanked me for helping her the other night—not that I did much apart from panic.' She shrugged and briefly met his gaze, and added with a smile that didn't reach her eyes, 'I figure I only have to be nice for her for another few months, then I'll probably never see her again.'

Lincoln held her gaze for a beat or two. 'You do like reminding me of the time frame on our marriage.'

And for some reason he didn't like being reminded—even though he was the one who'd put the timeframe there in the first place. Almost three weeks had already passed…soon it would be a month, then two, then three, and before he knew it he would be facing not only the death of his biological mother but the end of his relationship with Elodie.

He didn't know which he was dreading the most.

Elodie gave one of her sugar-sweet smiles. 'I wouldn't want either of us to get carried away because of all the fun we're having.'

He scooted closer to her on the sofa, reaching a hand to her face to stroke a lazy fingertip down the length of her cheek. 'I missed you.' His voice came out as rusty as a hinge on a centuries-old gate.

Something flickered in her gaze and the tip of her tongue slipped out to deposit a light sheen of moisture on her lips. 'I missed you too…' Her eyes lowered to his mouth and she snatched in a tiny breath.

Lincoln brought his mouth to hers, drawn to her with an almost unstoppable force. The softness of her lips beneath his sent a riot of sensations through his body. Heat, fire, throbbing lust. His kiss deepened, his blood thickened, his pulse quickened. His tongue met hers in a dance as old as time, a sexy salsa stirring his senses into manic overdrive.

He slid one of his hands along the side of her face, splaying his fingers against her scalp. Her lips responded to the pressure of his with equal passion and fervour, her soft moans of pleasure sending flames of heat through his body.

He lifted his mouth off hers, holding her face in his hands. 'How long have we got before dinner?'

Elodie stroked his jaw, her eyes shining with arousal, her lips curved in a sultry smile. 'How long do you need?'

'Not long.' Lincoln rose from the sofa and pulled her to her feet, settling his hands about her hips. 'We can save time by going to my study. I seem to remember you liked having fun in there…'

Her pupils flared and she nestled closer, the contact of her lower body sending a wave of powerful need through him that almost knocked him off his feet.

'Sounds like a plan.'

Elodie let Lincoln lead her to his study, a few doors down the long corridor. She went in before him, and once he was inside he closed the door and turned the key in the lock with a sharp click that sent a shiver racing down her spine.

She gave the room a sweeping glance, noting that it had also been redecorated, but stripped down rather than dressed up. It still had strong, masculine lines, with functional furniture—desk, chair and book-shelves and a modern lamp. There was a desktop computer, and a printer and scanner on a cabinet be-hind the desk. There were no items of sentimentality lying about, no photos or keepsakes. It was a reminder of the cool and clinical components to Lincoln's per-sonality—the inbuilt traits that made it difficult for him to show, let alone feel, sentiment or emotion.

'New office furniture...'

Elodie trailed a hand along the top of his desk. A flood of memories rushed through her mind. Erotic memories of desk sex after one of their legendary arguments. Was he recalling those red-hot episodes? Remembering the explosive passion that had flared between them?

She glanced at him and added, 'I suppose this desk's been used heaps of times?'

Lincoln came towards her, his eyes blazing with incendiary heat. 'Not the way we're about to use it.'

His hands gripped her by the hips again, and he lifted her so she was seated on his desk. Elodie linked her arms around his neck, gazing into the bluey-green kaleidoscope of his eyes. 'You mean you haven't christened it with anyone else?'

'No.'

She didn't like to read too much into his answer, but it surprised her all the same that he hadn't brought any of his lovers into this room. 'Why not?'

His mouth twisted in a rueful grimace. 'Lots of reasons.'

'Give me one.'

His gaze dipped to her mouth and then moved back to her eyes. 'I always associated this room with you. That's why I changed it. I couldn't look at the old desk without thinking of all the times we'd made love on it.'

Elodie brushed her mouth against his. 'I'll let you in on a little secret…' Her voice was little more than a whisper. 'I've only ever had desk sex with you.'

He stepped between her thighs and brought his mouth closer to hers. 'Does it make me sound like an egotist to be pleased about that?'

'Maybe a little.'

He smiled and closed the distance between their mouths in a searing kiss that made the hairs on the back of her neck tingle at the roots. His tongue entered her mouth with a silken thrust that set her blood on fire. Molten heat erupted between her legs, the heart of her womanhood swelling, moistening, aching and pulsing with primal need. His tongue tangled with hers in a dance of lust that made her desire for him escalate to a heart-stopping level.

He left her mouth after a few breathless moments, trailing his lips down the side of her neck to her bare skin, where her sweater had slipped off her shoulder. His hands lifted her sweater and she raised her arms like a child for him to haul it over her head. He tossed it to the floor behind him, then his hands were going to her leggings. She lifted her bottom off the desk to help him remove them from her body, her heart racing, her pulse pounding, her breath catching.

He devoured her with his hungry eyes, his hands running over the globes of her lace-covered breasts with toe-curling expertise. 'I want you naked.' His tone was deep and husky.

'And so you shall have me…once we get things a little more even around here.'

Elodie began to undo the buttons on his business shirt, but she'd only got to the third one when he became impatient. With a grunt, he took over the job, stripping his shirt off and sending it in the same direction as her sweater. She slid her hands over his well-defined pectoral muscles, her blood ticking with excitement. She brought her mouth to his chest, licking with her tongue across each of his flat male nipples, then circling them in turn.

He drew in a ragged breath and placed his hands on the fastener at the back of her bra, deftly unclipping it. He lowered his mouth to her right breast, caressing the tightly budded nipple with his lips and tongue. Need throbbed in every cell of her body, the sensations he was evoking making her breath catch in her throat. He opened his mouth over her nipple and drew on the sensitised flesh, the sucking motion triggering a firestorm in her lower body. Then he moved to her other breast, teasing it into the same sensual raptures, the rasp of his tongue, the gentle graze of his teeth making her pant with longing.

Elodie worked blindly on the waistband of his trousers, desperate to get her hands on him, but he was too intent on pleasuring her. He pushed her back on the desk, pulling her knickers off her with one hand and tossing them to the floor. His mouth came down to her abdomen, his tongue tracing a light teasing circle around her belly button. Shivers coursed up and down her spine and a wave of tingling heat and tension found its way to her core.

His mouth moved down to the heart of her, his lips and tongue separating her folds, all too soon sending her into a freefall of mind-blowing, earth-shattering, dizzying release. She arched her spine, riding out the pulsating waves, unable to control her whimpering cries and panting breaths.

'Wow, oh, wow…' There were no words to describe the bliss still reverberating through her in delicious little aftershocks. But she finally sat upright and reached for him. 'My turn to render you speechless, I think. But we have to get you out of those trousers first.'

'That's easily fixed.'

Lincoln's gaze ran over her flushed features, his eyes smouldering, and he dropped his trousers and his underwear. He moved away briefly, to get a condom from the wallet in his trouser pocket, applying it and coming back to her.

She never got tired of looking at him naked. His lean, athletic build was wonderfully proportioned—

toned muscles, broad shoulders, slim hips, long, strong legs.

Elodie slipped off the desk and pushed him down so his back was against it. She slithered down in front of him, caressing him with her hands first, enjoying the guttural sounds of his pleasure. Then she placed her mouth on him, using her lips and tongue to bring him to the point of no return. He shuddered and groaned and swore under her ministrations, his body finally going slack as the last wave of release flowed through him.

'You really know how to bring me to my knees...' His voice was rough around the edges, his breathing hectic. 'I'm not sure I can stand upright just yet.'

Elodie came up to stroke her hands over his muscular chest. 'My legs are still shaking too.'

He cupped one side of her face in his hand, his eyes holding hers with glittering intensity. 'We'd better not make Morag wait too long to serve dinner, but first I want to do this.'

He brought his mouth down to hers in a long, slow kiss that drugged her senses all over again. It was passionate, and yet surprisingly tender, a kiss that stirred her emotions and fuelled her hopes.

Was it crazy to hope he was becoming as invested in their relationship as she was? Was she a fool for hoping he was moving past the bitterness he had carried against for her the last seven years?

CHAPTER ELEVEN

A COUPLE OF days before they were due to attend El-speth and Mack's wedding in the Highlands of Scot-land, Lincoln informed Elodie over breakfast that they would have to travel separately, due to an urgent work issue that had cropped up.

Elodie put her cup of tea down and frowned. 'But what if you get held up? We're supposed to be there together. Won't it look odd if we're not?'

'I'll get there—don't worry.' He buttered his toast with a brisk scrape of his knife, the scratching sound loud in the silence. A frown was carved into his fore-head, his eyes narrowed in concentration.

'Will you find it…triggering? I mean, being at a traditional wedding?'

He put his knife down with a little clatter against his plate. 'I've been to a few since—so, no, I won't be triggered.' He arched one dark brow and added, 'Will you?'

She bit her lip and picked up her cup again, cra-dling it in her hands. 'I'm trying not to think about it…'

'How's that working for you?'

'Not well. I feel sick already.'

It was true. She had woken up for the last three days with grumbling nausea, which she'd put down to the anxiety of attending a wedding so similar to her original one.

Lincoln sighed and reached for her hand across the table. 'What's worrying you specifically?'

She shrugged and lowered her cup to the table again. 'I don't want to spoil Elspeth and Mack's special day by drawing any attention to myself. You know what the press are like.'

'Is it because you'll be seeing Fraser MacDiarmid there?'

Elodie grimaced. 'That and other things.'

'What other things?'

She whooshed out a sigh. 'I'm sorry... I'm probably overthinking it all.'

He squeezed her hand, his concerned gaze focussed on hers. 'Sweetheart, talk to me. What is it about attending the wedding that worries you the most?'

Elodie blinked back the sting of sudden tears. Along with the nausea, her emotions were all over the place lately. 'I don't know...it's just the thought of getting ready with Elspeth and the other bridesmaids. It makes me...unsettled. I keep thinking about *our* wedding day—how I suppressed my doubts and fears all the way through the preparations. I sat there with Elspeth and the other girls, pretending to be the blissfully happy bride...'

She gulped and then continued.

'I didn't realise I was going to do a no-show until I was a block away from the church. And then I—I panicked. Like a full-on panic attack. I couldn't breathe, I was shaking, sweating, nauseous. I felt an overwhelming need to get away as quickly as I could. On one level I guess I knew the scandal and hurt it would cause, but right then and there I didn't care. I had to get away.'

Lincoln's hand was stroking hers in a soothing fashion. 'Listen to me.' His tóne was as calming and stabilising as his touch. 'I'll be with you at Elspeth and Mack's wedding. I'll reschedule my meeting for next week so we can travel together. I'll help you get through it, every step of the way.'

Elodie met his gaze with her watery one. 'I'm sorry for what I did to you back then. I'm sorry I wasn't mature enough to recognise what I felt until it was too late.'

Lincoln gave a wry smile and squeezed her hand once more. 'It's in the past. We need to move on from it.'

But had he truly moved on? This six-month marriage deal was hardly what anyone could call a moving-on plan. He had once promised her so much more and she had thrown it away. He wasn't offering her a second chance. Their relationship was an interim thing to help comfort his biological mother in her final months of life.

And even though they were only a month into their marriage, Elodie could hear the clock ticking. Loudly.

* * *

'Oh, you look so beautiful,' Elodie said, standing in front of her twin the day of the wedding. 'And I don't think I've ever seen you look so happy. You're positively glowing.'

Elspeth grasped one of Elodie's hands in excitement. 'I'm so happy I could burst.' Then her expression sobered. 'But how are *you*? You don't seem yourself at all. And you haven't touched your glass of champagne.'

Elodie adjusted the right sleeve of her twin's wedding gown. 'I'm fine.' She gave a tight little smile. 'Just a little nervous.'

'Because of seeing Fraser? Don't be. He's done some work on himself and is quite pleasant to be around these days.'

'I'm glad to hear it but, no, it's not about him.'

Elspeth peered at her a little more closely. 'How are things with Lincoln?'

'Fine.'

'Just "fine"?'

Elodie drew in a skittering breath. Even the mention of his name was enough to get her heart racing. He had been so tender and attentive on their journey to Scotland, no one would ever think they were not the real deal, that their marriage was a temporary arrangement.

'He's wonderful.' She sighed and continued, 'So wonderful I keep having to remind myself we're only staying together another few months.'

'You want more?'

Elodie smoothed her hands down her own beautiful dress and sighed. 'Yes, well…haven't I always wanted more? More than he's prepared to give me, that is. Sometimes I think he's developing stronger feelings for me, but what if I'm wrong? It's not exactly something I can ask him. *Hey, honey, do you love me?* I'm not sure that's going to go down well, given the terms he insisted on for our marriage.'

Elspeth grasped both of Elodie's hands. 'I've always thought Lincoln has strong feelings for you. But I don't like to offer you false hope in case I'm wrong. All I can say is be patient with him. Some men take a while to recognise their own feelings.'

Would six months be long enough? Or would she end up bitterly disappointed in the end?

Elodie gave a rueful smile. 'I'd give you a hug, but I don't want to crush your dress.'

Elspeth pulled her into a big squishy hug regardless. 'Love you.'

'Love you back.' Elodie pulled away to look at her twin. 'Are you disappointed Dad isn't here to give you away?'

'Not really. My days of being disappointed by Dad are well and truly over. Besides, I have all I need in terms of love from Mack. And I really like Mum's partner, Jim. He's stable and reliable and so supportive of her.'

Elodie couldn't help thinking she was the only one in her family without the security of knowing her partner truly loved her.

But her twin was convinced Lincoln had done so once.

If so, could he do it again?

Lincoln wasn't part of the bridal party, so he took a seat along with the other guests in the local kirk. It being late autumn, the bridal couple had decided against a garden wedding at Mack's ancestral home, Crannochbrae, but the reception would be held there in the castle. It was also where Lincoln and Elodie were staying, along with other members of the bridal party and close family.

He hadn't seen much of Elodie since they'd arrived, as she was busy helping her twin prepare for her big day. But nothing could have prepared him for seeing her walk down the aisle as the first of the three bridesmaids. He stood along with the other guests, watching her take each step towards the front of the church.

He had said he wouldn't be triggered, but how could he not be? He remembered all too well the air of expectation that day seven years ago. And then the flicker of unease when the time had kept creeping past. He remembered the increasing murmurs of the congregation, the worried glances towards the back of the cathedral. The glances that had then settled on him, standing at the front with his groomsmen. He remembered the slow crawl of humiliation travelling over his skin when he'd considered the possibility that Elodie wasn't coming.

He recalled the moment when someone at the back of the cathedral had been passed a note, and how he'd come towards him, taking so long it had felt like a decade before he'd got to him. He'd taken the note and looked at it blindly, for endless seconds. It had been from the driver who was supposed to have delivered Elodie to the cathedral, informing him that she had bolted.

Lincoln pulled himself out of the past to look at Elodie coming towards him now. Dressed in a close-fitting cobalt blue satin dress that hugged every delicious curve of her body, her face beautifully made up, her hair in a sophisticated updo that highlighted her aristocratic features and swan-like neck, she was carrying a posy of fresh flowers with long flowing ribbons the same colour as her dress.

She glanced at him with a tremulous smile and he smiled back, sending her a wink for good measure. A light blush stained her cheeks and she continued walking up the aisle. He drank in the back view of her before the next bridesmaid came past. And then he watched as the bride came past, so uncannily like Elodie that it triggered him all over again.

The ceremony began and Lincoln listened to the words, watching the rituals and traditions with an uneasy sensation in his gut. Not because he didn't think they were genuine or worthwhile, but because his recent marriage ceremony to Elodie couldn't have been more different.

Was she feeling the same? Were the heartfelt words

and vows and promises and the devoted looks the bridal couple were exchanging making her feel a little short-changed?

But he had been up-front with her about what he expected of their marriage. It was for six months and six months only. One month had already passed. They had five months to go and then it would be over. They would both be free to move on with their lives.

And hopefully, by then, he'd be able to go to any number of weddings and not be triggered at all.

Elodie smiled her way through the official photos, and continued to smile and chat to the others in the bridal party, but all she could think about was how sterile and clinical her wedding to Lincoln had been a month before. Watching Elspeth and Mack gaze into each other's eyes with such devotion had made her ache with envy. If only Lincoln loved her the way she loved him. Had *always* loved him. But her love now was a more mature love—a love that had grown up, letting her recognise her own failings in their previous relationship and how she had to be aware of not falling into old patterns of behaviour.

As she was on the bridal table, she wasn't able to be with Lincoln until the formal part of the reception was over. Then he came over to her with a smile, holding out his hand to her. 'Dance with me?'

Elodie took his hand and joined him on the dance floor in a slow waltz. 'Has it been absolutely dreadful for you on the table with all my rowdy cousins?' she asked.

'Not at all. I had a great vantage point from there to watch you all night.'

'I noticed you looking at me a few times.'

More than a few times. It seemed every time she'd looked his way he'd been looking at her. But then, she'd had trouble keeping her eyes from drifting his way too.

His eyes glinted. 'How could I not notice the most beautiful woman in the room?'

Elodie gave a twisted smile. 'I'm not sure Mack would agree with you on that.' She sighed and, focussing her gaze on the neat knot of his tie, added, 'It was a lovely service. I had trouble controlling the urge to cry.'

Lincoln tipped up her chin with his hand, meshing his gaze with hers. 'Are you disappointed that our wedding last month was the complete opposite?'

She stripped her features of all emotion. 'Why would I be? We agreed on the terms.'

He studied her for a long beat. 'All the same, I could have made it a little less sterile.' There was a note of regret in his tone and a small frown pulled at his brow.

'But we don't have the same kind of relationship as Els and Mack.'

'Perhaps not.' He gave an on-off smile that didn't have time to reach his eyes. 'But then are any two relationships the same? Take us, for instance. Our first relationship was different from what we have now.'

'Do you think so?'

He turned her away from another couple who were getting a little close, his hold warm and protective. 'We talk more now. We don't argue as much. And making love with you is even more exciting and satisfying.'

'Even without the arguments?'

He smiled and brought her right hand up to his mouth. 'I do kind of miss those arguments.'

Elodie gave a sheepish smile. 'Yes, well…we both have strong wills and seem to clash on just about everything.' Her smile faded and she continued with a tiny frown, 'Makes me wonder why we got together in the first place. Our relationship was totally based on lust. I'm not sure it's the best foundation for a lasting union.'

The hand resting on the small of her back pressed her a little closer to the hot, hard heat of his body. 'It's a damn good starting point, though.' He lowered his head so his breath mingled intimately with hers. 'How soon can we go upstairs?'

Desire licked at her with searing tongues of flame. 'Not until the bride and groom leave.'

'How long will that be?' There was an impatient groan in his voice, and he lowered his mouth closer to her.

Elodie smiled against his lips. 'Too long. But I'm sure, knowing you, it will be well and truly worth the wait.'

And it was.

* * *

Elodie woke the following morning with a dizzying wave of nausea. Lincoln was still asleep beside her, one of his arms lying across her body.

She swallowed back the rising bile in her throat and gently eased out of his relaxed hold. She got to her feet and walked carefully to the en suite bathroom, her stomach churning, her mouth dry, her fingertips tingling as if her blood pressure was dropping. She made it to the toilet in time to release the contents of her stomach, but unfortunately there was no way to do so without making a noise.

Lincoln opened the bathroom door and rushed over to her. 'Sweetheart, are you okay?'

Elodie groaned and shook her head. 'Go away. I'll be fine in a minute.'

He pulled her hair back from her face, then reached for a facecloth and handed it to her. 'You must've had too much to drink last night.'

'I didn't drink at all… I—I think it's a stomach virus. I've been feeling a little off for a couple of days.'

'Why didn't you tell me?'

Elodie stayed hunched over the toilet, not quite confident that her stomach was settled enough for her to move. 'Please, just leave me to deal with this. I don't need an audience right now.'

Lincoln flushed the toilet and then crouched down beside her, his expression full of concern. 'I'm not leaving you. What if you pass out and knock yourself out or something?' He put a hand to her forehead. 'You don't seem to have a temperature, but you're clammy.' He lowered his hand from her face and straightened to get another facecloth, this time rinsing it under the tap first. He crouched back down beside her and handed it to her. 'Here.'

'Thanks…' Elodie dabbed at her face, then handed it back to him. 'I think I'll be okay now.'

'Here, let me help you up.' Lincoln took her gently by the shoulders and guided her to a standing position. 'Do you feel up to having a shower?'

'Yes… I think so.'

'I'll stay with you.'

Elodie would have argued the point, but she was still feeling a little light-headed. Or maybe that was because he was naked and looking as gorgeously sexy as ever. She brushed her teeth and rinsed, relieved the bout of hideous nausea had passed.

Lincoln turned the shower on for her and helped her in.

'Aren't you going to join me?' she asked.

'Only to help you shower. Nothing else.'

He stepped under the spray of water with her, making sure not to take the bulk of the flow away from her. He shampooed her hair, gently massaging her scalp, then rinsed it and applied conditioner before repeating the massage. She was very conscious of his lean, athletic body so close to hers, wet and naked… and aroused.

'That feels divine…' She sighed and turned so she was facing him. Her hands settled on his slim hips and she moved closer to the jut of his erection. 'So does that…'

Lincoln placed his hands on her shoulders. 'I didn't get in the shower to have sex with you. You're not feeling well.'

'But I'm fine now.' Elodie pressed herself against him and he groaned. 'And you want me.'

'I can wait. I want to make sure you're feeling a hundred percent first.' He placed a soft-as-air kiss on the top of her damp shoulder.

Elodie stroked her hands down his chest, her heart skipping a beat at the tender look in his eyes. 'Thanks for making me feel better.'

He brushed her lips with his. 'Glad to be of help.' He turned off the shower and stepped out, picking up one of the bath sheets from the towel rail and holding it out for her. 'Come here and let me dry you.'

Elodie stepped into the warm folds of the towel and he proceeded to dry her. It was a thing he had never done, and it shifted something in their relationship. She had never allowed herself to be so vulnerable before. Seven years ago she would never have allowed him to see her hunched over a toilet bowl being sick, or bent double with period pain…

Period pain.

An invisible hammer swung against her heart, knocking it sideways in her chest. When was the last time she'd had a period?

She gave a jolt and Lincoln looked up from drying her feet.

'Sorry, was I too rough?'

Elodie stared down at him, kneeling at her feet, her mind whirling with dawning realisation. The nausea. The dizziness. The light-headedness. The sudden aversion to things she usually enjoyed, like champagne.

She swallowed and somehow got her voice to work. 'No…no… I was just getting a little cold.' She was, in fact, now shivering. Shivering with alarm. Panic. Despair.

How could she be pregnant? They had used condoms every time. Lincoln was pedantic about safety—it was something she admired about him. He would never intentionally put her or indeed any of his partners at risk.

Lincoln straightened and wrapped her in a fresh towel, warm from the towel rail. 'Go back to bed for a while. I can change our flights to London to a later time.'

'No, it's okay. I want to get back to work tomorrow.'

And get her hands on a pregnancy test as soon as possible.

CHAPTER TWELVE

LINCOLN WAS AWARE of Elodie's silence on the way back to London. She kept assuring him she was feeling fine, but he wasn't so sure. In the past, he would have been fooled by her assurances, but this time he wasn't. She still looked pale, and she was huddled into herself as if she was in pain.

He knew from experience that a stomach virus could knock you sideways, leaving you listless and wan for days... He put his arm around her on the way to the car once they had landed in London. 'I think we should get you to a doctor for a check-up, just to make sure you're okay.'

Elodie pulled out of his embrace with a jerk that caught him off-guard. 'Will you stop fussing? I told you I'm fine. I'm just tired from all the travelling.'

Her tone was sharp and impatient, but her expression didn't match. There was a nervous flicker in her eyes and she didn't seem to want to meet his gaze at all.

He decided against pressuring her. That was another thing he knew from experience—she didn't take kindly to being told what to do.

The journey was mostly silent on the way to his house, but a few blocks before they got home Elodie asked if he would mind stopping while she picked up something at the local pharmacy.

'What do you need?'

'Just…female stuff.' Her voice was little more than a mumble.

For a young woman who had spent years parading on catwalks in the skimpiest underwear and swim-wear, Elodie could be surprising prudish about her monthly period.

Lincoln pulled into the next available parking space and turned off the engine. 'Do you want me to go in for you?'

She reared back, as if he had suggested he walk into the pharmacy buck naked. 'No. I'll go. I won't be long.'

She scurried out of the car before he could open the door for her and shut it behind her.

Lincoln waited on the footpath, holding the door open for her when she returned a couple of minutes later. She was carrying a paper bag in her hand and her head was down, her cheeks filled with more co-lour than he had seen in them for hours. She slipped into the seat and flashed him a *thank you* smile that didn't make the full distance to her eyes.

Lincoln resumed the driver's seat and continued on the journey home. He parked outside his house and turned off the engine. 'I guess I should be feeling relieved you need those.' He glanced at the package she was holding.

'What?' She looked at him blankly, her forehead still knitted with a frown.

'Tampons and pads.'

'Oh…right…yes…'

He flicked her another glance, but she was looking out of the side window. 'Elodie?'

'What?'

Her voice was little more than a croak, and she still didn't look his way. But he noticed how tight her grip was on the package she was holding—the paper bag was crackling as if she was crushing crisps.

'You don't have to be shy about having your period. I did grow up with a sister, you know.'

The paper bag went silent and she turned to look at him. 'I'm not having my period.'

There was a strange quality to her voice…an empty, hollow sound that sent a ghostly shiver across the back of his neck.

'This is a pregnancy test.'

Lincoln stared at her with his mouth open, his heart beating like a drum set on some weird staccato rhythm. He could barely think about having a baby without a wave of panic coursing through him. He was to be a *father*?

He hadn't considered the possibility for years. Seven years, in fact. He had once wanted a family like the one he had grown up in, but Elodie jilting him had made him reset his goals. When she hadn't shown up at the church that day, everything had changed for him. He hadn't been able to imagine wanting a family with anyone else. He had taught himself to be content with the thought of being an uncle to his siblings' children rather than long for a dream he had lost and couldn't get back.

But if Elodie was carrying his child…

'You think you might be *pregnant*?'

'I'm not sure…' She swallowed and continued, 'I've got some symptoms. I've had some bouts of nausea and I'm late.'

'How late?'

'A few days…almost a week.'

Lincoln looked at the package in her hands. 'We'd better go in and do the test. The sooner we know, the sooner we can plan what to do.'

He got out of the car and came around to her side, opening the door for her. She alighted from the car and looked up at him with a frown.

'What do you mean "plan"?'

He closed the door with a snap and took her by the elbow. 'A pregnancy would change everything. We'd have to shift the goalposts on our marriage. We'd have to take out the six-months clause and make it permanent.'

Elodie tugged out of his hold. 'Will you stop railroading me, for God's sake? I don't even know if I'm pregnant. We've been using condoms all the time.'

There was a beat or two of silence. Lincoln could hear his heart thumping and his stomach dropped. 'Is there a possibility it's someone else's?'

Her face blanched of colour and she pushed past

him to go to the front door. Lincoln let out a curse and followed her. He opened the door and she stalked inside and made her way straight up the stairs.

'Elodie, you know I had to ask you that, right?' Even to his ears, his voice sounded hoarse.

She turned on the fourth stair to look at him. 'I know you did, but can we just wait until we see what the test says?'

'Sure.' He scraped a hand through his hair and sighed so heavily he was surprised the draught of his breath didn't knock over the hall table.

Elodie ran the rest of the way up the stairs to the nearest bathroom, closing and locking the door behind her. She stared at the package in her hand, her heart hammering as if she'd run up five flights of stairs instead of just one.

She ripped open the bag and the packaging and quickly read the instructions. She performed the test as outlined and waited for the result.

The first minute ticked by with agonising slowness, intensifying her distress.

If she was pregnant, Lincoln would want to stay married to her because of the baby—not because of her. Not because he loved *her*, but because he wanted his baby to have an active and involved father.

The second minute ticked past and her heart rate sped up.

She stared at the wand in her hand, not sure what she wanted to see.

The ambiguity of her feelings shocked her. She had

thought she wasn't the maternal type; her biological clock hadn't made a sound—ever. But now, as she waited for the lines to appear, she thought about the possibility of a baby. Lincoln's baby.

The third minute passed, and then the fourth.

Elodie was trying to keep the wand steady enough to read it. The instructions had said to give the test a good window of time—five to ten minutes at least. She didn't know how to deal with the suspense. Everything depended on the results of the test.

Finally, ten minutes passed and she held the wand up to the light. *Negative.* She waited another minute, her heart so tight in her chest she could barely take a breath. A wave of disappointment ambushed her. She wasn't carrying Lincoln's baby. There was no pregnancy. No need to change the terms of their marriage.

No need for her to stay with him…unless he loved her.

Elodie put the packaging in the bin but kept the wand, knowing Lincoln would insist on seeing it for himself. She didn't have to call him upstairs for he was waiting outside the bathroom door, with an unreadable expression on his face.

'How did it go?' His voice held no trace of worry, anxiety or fear.

'It's negative.' She showed him the wand.

He peered at it, his brow furrowed. 'Are you sure?'

'I gave it more than ample time to develop. It's negative. I'm not pregnant.'

He met her gaze. 'Are you relieved or disappointed?'

'To be honest, I'm a bit of both.'

She went back into the bathroom and put the wand in the bin. She washed her hands and gave herself a quick glance in the mirror, but it was like looking at a different person from the one she'd been just ten minutes ago.

The before-the-pregnancy-test Elodie had not been the earth mother type. A baby was something other people had. It wasn't on her radar. Her business was her baby. Her design label was still in its infancy. It hadn't had time to develop and grow and become successful.

But the post-negative-pregnancy-test Elodie wanted to carry Lincoln's baby in her womb, to give birth to it with him by her side, to raise it with him in a household full of love. But wasn't that little more than a foolish dream?

Lincoln was still standing outside the bathroom when she came out again. 'I think we need to talk.'

Elodie gave him a stiff smile. 'Yes, we do.' She let out a long breath and met his gaze once more. 'Why did you offer to make our marriage permanent if I was pregnant?'

'Because it would have been the right thing to do. I want any child of mine to have my name, and to bring it up like I was brought up—in a loving home. Even if the baby hadn't been mine, I would still have married you to give it a loving home.'

'But ours wouldn't be a loving home, would it? I mean, we would love our child, but what about each other?'

Lincoln's throat moved up and down. 'You have feelings for me, don't you?'

'It's not my feelings I'm most worried about. It's yours.'

'You know I care about you.'

'But you're not in love with me. Not now, and not seven years ago. So we've basically come full circle.'

There was a thick beat of silence.

Lincoln set his jaw. 'What do you mean by that? We have an agreement. There's a lot riding on it. Nina, your label, the funds I've put up for you… We have five months left.'

'For me to do what? Make passionate love with you but never hear you say the words I most want to hear? I want someone to love me—not for how I look or how good I am in bed or whether I'm pregnant or not. *Me*.' She banged her hand against her chest for emphasis. 'Me, with all my faults and foibles. That's what I want from you. But you can't or won't give it to me.'

He scraped a hand through his hair, his eyes flicking away from hers before coming back with glittering intensity. 'Are you saying you're in love with me?'

'Don't look so surprised!' Elodie gave a cynical laugh that was nowhere in the vicinity of humour. 'You make it so damn hard *not* to fall in love with you. But it's not enough for me to stay with you. I'm not wasting another five months of my life waiting for you to feel something for me other than physical attraction. That makes you no different from thousands, probably millions of other men out there who feel the same way about me.'

She dropped her shoulders on a sigh and then went on.

'I get it—I really do. You have bonding issues that probably go way back to infancy. You were adopted—and, while it was a good adoption, you still carry the wound of being relinquished at birth, even if it's only on a subconscious level. You don't let people get close to you. You don't let them in. You don't show your vulnerability.'

Lincoln's features were set in stone. 'If you leave, the deal is off. I'll withdraw my financial support for your label.'

Elodie brushed past him to go back to the master bedroom and collect her things. 'Do it. See if I care. I'll find someone else.'

'Where are you going? Talk to me, for God's sake.'

She swung around to face him. 'Tell me what you're feeling right now.'

He frowned so hard his eyebrows met above the bridge of his nose. 'I'm angry you're running away again without talking this through. You're acting like a spoilt child.'

'I'm not being childish this time. Last time I was running away from myself more than I was running away from you. I couldn't even face up to the truth about myself back then, so how could I tell you? But I'm telling you now. I can't be with you because we don't want the same things out of life. You essentially want a six-month fling with me. Do you think

I can't hear the clock ticking on our relationship? You put timelines on all your relationships because every woman you've cared about has left you. Your birth mother...your adoptive mother. And it's why you won't let your housekeeper go in spite of her appalling behaviour towards me in the past.'

'We can extend the time. I'm fine with that. We can keep it open and—'

'And what? A year on, two years or more, I'll still be waiting for you to fall in love with me. I'm not doing it, Lincoln. I want out. The pregnancy scare has jolted me into reality. *My* reality. Which is that I deserve to be loved for me. Just me.'

'Is this because I asked if the baby was mine?'

'No. You had an absolute right to ask that question under the circumstances. The press have made me out to be a female version of a playboy.' She sighed again, and added, 'I've spent years of my life pretending I don't care what people think of me, but deep down I do care. I've always cared. But I've buried those feelings so deep down they come out in other ways—such as in stupid and impulsive behaviour.'

'I don't want you to leave.' There was a raw quality to his voice. 'Stay a little longer. You might see things differently once you've got over the shock of thinking you were pregnant.'

Elodie went up to him and placed a hand on his lean jaw. 'Here's the thing that's shocking. A part of me wanted to be pregnant.'

He blinked a couple of times, his Adam's apple

rising and falling. 'Then you can get pregnant. We'll stop using condoms and—'

She placed her finger over his lips, blocking the rest of his speech. 'No. Listen to me. I've worked so hard to form my own label. It's almost within my grasp and I can't let anything stop me now. If I have a baby with someone it will be in a couple of years, not now.' She lowered her hand from his face and stepped back with a sad smile. 'It's time for me to leave. I know you don't want things to end this way, but I think it's for the best. Please send my best wishes to Nina. I'll pop a letter in the post for her.'

'This is crazy, Elodie. You're not thinking clearly and—'

'It's not just about the pregnancy scare. Elspeth and Mack's wedding really got to me as well. I'm so envious of what they have together. I fooled myself into thinking we could be like them, but it's not possible. I see that now. And I saw it seven years ago.'

'I suppose I should be grateful for the luxury of watching you pack up and leave this time.' The stinging sarcasm in his tone was unmistakable.

'You can watch me if you like. But I'd like us to part on better terms.' She took another few steps towards the bedroom before stopping and turning around again. She took off her wedding and engagement rings and handed them to him. 'Here—just in case anything goes astray again.'

He didn't even glance at the rings. 'I don't want them.'

Elodie closed her fingers over the rings. 'I'll leave them on the hall table, like last time.'

But he had already turned and walked away, and she didn't know if he had heard her or not.

Even if Lincoln hadn't heard the sounds of Elodie leaving his house, he knew he would have sensed the exact moment she'd gone. The house was different without her. The energy, the atmosphere faded away to a bland nothingness.

He considered moving to another bedroom, so he didn't have to be reminded of her, or going to a hotel for a while. He didn't want to smell the lingering trace of her perfume or picture her lying in his bed with her red-gold hair spread all over the pillow. To be tortured by every memory of their month together living as man and wife.

To say he was blindsided was an understatement, but the pregnancy scare had thrown him right out of kilter. He still couldn't get his still spinning head wrapped around the negative result. He'd got himself so worked up, so focussed on doing the right thing by Elodie and the baby, it had taken him a while to realise there was no baby.

But it wasn't only the pregnancy scare that had thrown him. He hadn't been expecting her to walk out—not before their time was up. He was the one who was supposed to call time on their relationship, not her.

There was no way of keeping Elodie married to him unless he said the words she wanted to hear. His feelings for her were complex, and messy, and he didn't like thinking too deeply about them. They got him tied up in knots—gnarly knots that pulled on his organs to the point of pain. She made him feel out of control—not just in terms of passion but in terms of vulnerability.

To openly confess to loving someone you had to accept that they could hurt you, leave you, sabotage you…humiliate you. And hadn't Elodie done all that? He had spent the last seven years trying to block every thought of her from his mind. She fancied herself in love with him, but how could he be sure it wasn't just because of the financial help he had given her for her label? A gift of money had a way of triggering all sorts of strong feelings.

He walked past the hall table and saw her wedding and engagement rings lying there. He picked them up, staring at them for a long moment.

How could one woman wreak such havoc in his life? What gave her the power to make his gut churn at the thought of never seeing her again? Or, worse, seeing her with someone else? Someone else who would father her future baby. The baby she'd decided she wanted in the not too distant future.

He tossed the rings back on the table and turned away. Maybe a month in a hotel would be a good idea.

A hotel a long way from London.

Elodie didn't want to spoil her twin's honeymoon, so left it another week before she called her about her breakup with Lincoln.

Elspeth was sympathetic and understanding of Elodie's decision to leave, and offered whatever support she needed.

'Have you seen or talked to him since?'

'No. I think it's best not to. A clean break is better.'

'I guess so…' There was more than a speck of doubt in Elspeth's tone.

'I *know* so,' Elodie said with conviction. 'He's never really forgiven me for leaving him the first time. I'm annoyed at myself for even considering it might work between us. What was I thinking? I should've had better sense. He didn't love me before. He doesn't love me now. I have to accept he's never going to.'

And the sooner she got on with her life without him, the better.

Lincoln came back to his London house after a month of working in New York. Well, trying to work… He'd come down with the same stomach virus Elodie had had in Scotland and it had only intensified his misery.

Like the last time Elodie had left, he'd given his housekeeper strict instructions to remove every trace of her from the house while he was away. But he'd more or less given up trying not to think about her. She was in his thoughts day and night, torturing him with memories of her touch, her smile, her playfulness. And coming home made it even worse.

His house was so empty without her. His life was so empty without her.

His coping strategy in life was always to keep

busy. He worked hard, played hard. He didn't have time for soft and fuzzy emotions. They didn't belong in his world of tough decision-making, wheeling and dealing and keeping an eye out for the next big challenge.

Elodie was the biggest challenge of his life and he had let her go.

He had lost her not once, but twice.

Lincoln wanted Elodie back and he hated himself for it.

He should have moved on by now. He should have moved on seven years ago. But he was stuck on her.

He would have to get unstuck soon, or he would be living the rest of his life as a monk. The thought of sleeping with anyone else made his stomach churn. He hadn't even looked at another woman while he was in New York. No one had turned his head or stopped his heart. The busiest city in the world hadn't held its usual appeal. He hadn't even enjoyed the deals he'd set up—in fact, the whole time he'd been bored. Empty and unfulfilled.

He wanted *her*. Only her.

Elodie was his nemesis—the one person who could make him feel things he had never wanted to feel for anyone. Was that love? Did he have this empty, aching feeling in his chest because he loved her and wanted her back so badly he couldn't think straight?

He still loved her.

Acknowledging the truth of those words was like suddenly remembering a language he had taught himself not to speak for years. But now he wanted to shout the words out loud.

I love her. I love her. I love her.

Morag appeared from the kitchen to greet him. 'How was your trip?'

'Awful.'

'I'm sorry…' Her gaze slipped away from his. 'Have you heard from Elodie?'

'No.'

Even hearing her name twisted a knife into his gut. What if she didn't believe him when he went to see her? He hadn't exactly given her a reason to harbour any hope that he might change his mind. The thing was, he *hadn't* changed his mind. His mind had finally revealed to him what he had been hiding from all these years.

He. Loved. Her.

'There's something I need to tell you about the last time Elodie left,' Morag said. 'I'm afraid you're not going to like hearing it.'

Lincoln frowned. 'Go on.'

Morag twisted her hands in front of her apron. 'She was telling the truth when she told you she left her engagement ring on the hall table. I found it.'

'Where is it now?'

Morag took something out of the pocket on the front of her apron and handed it to him. He stared at the ring box, his mind whirling. He hadn't believed Elodie about the ring. He had always thought she'd sold it and used the money to launch her career. He'd been so blind and prejudiced against her… Had he ever truly listened to her? Understood her? Believed in her?

He had kept her at arm's length, determined not to let her see how much he needed her, how much he loved her. How much it frightened and terrified him to love her, to openly admit it, to own it and say it out loud. He had always blamed Elodie for leaving him—but he had left first. In fact, he hadn't been there emotionally in the first place. Not totally, not unreservedly.

He looked back at his housekeeper. 'Why didn't you tell me she'd left it seven years ago?'

'I tried to, but you came back roaring drunk the night after she jilted you and you refused to have her name even mentioned in your presence. You told me to remove everything of hers from the house, just as you did this time.'

Lincoln could recall most of that conversation—most, but not all. Which wasn't something that made him particularly proud. 'Why didn't you tell me when I was in a better state of mind?'

'I thought about it that night, and the next day while you were sleeping off your hangover. I thought if I told you she'd left it behind you might go and find her, talk her into coming back to you.' Morag gulped back a broken sound. 'I didn't think she loved you, so I didn't tell you. But I was wrong. She did—she does. I think she always will.'

Lincoln's heart leapt right up to his throat. Could it be possible Elodie truly loved him? That it wasn't too late to undo the damage of his past mistakes and miscommunications? She had more to forgive of him than he ever had for her. Dared he hope she would find it in her heart to take him back?

'Does she know you have the ring?'

'She found it when she was looking for my insulin kit. She could've told you she'd found it that night, but she didn't. I think because she didn't want you to be hurt by my betrayal of your trust. And then, once I realised she knew, I begged her not to tell you. I shouldn't have asked her to do that for me. I'm worried it's contributed to your breakup.'

A rush of love and respect coursed through him for his beautiful Elodie. But she was no longer his—not unless he went to her and told her how he felt. How he had *always* felt.

'I need to see her. I was going anyway, so it has nothing to do with the ring.' He pocketed the ring and placed a hand on Morag's shoulder. 'You're not to blame for this. I am. I should've told her seven years ago what I felt for her.'

Morag's face lit up like a chandelier. 'You mean you love her?'

Lincoln smiled. 'You bet I do.'

Elodie was working late in her studio, doing some last touches on the collection of clothes she'd made for Nina. She had got Nina's measurements during a phone conversation with her, after she'd explained her reasons for leaving Lincoln. It had been a tough conversation to have—especially knowing of Nina's physical fragility—but Elodie had no longer been able to pretend. It was time to be honest about all things—most of all her feelings about the only man she had ever loved.

She was spreading out the last item of the collection on her work table when she caught sight of movement on the security camera covering the front door of the studio. She put the dress down and went closer to the security screen, her heart bouncing up and down in her chest like a yo-yo.

Lincoln was standing outside the studio, looking for a doorbell that didn't yet exist. His brow was furrowed and he kept reaching up to tug at his tie, as if it were choking him. He glanced up to the second floor, where she was working, but she wasn't near the window so he couldn't see her.

Elodie stepped away from the security camera and went over to the window. She unlocked it and opened it, bracing herself for an icy blast of the wintry night air. 'Lincoln?'

He looked up with relief flooding his features. 'I need to talk to you. Can I come up?'

His voice sounded rough around the edges, even from this height, and she could see the lines of strain and stress around his mouth.

'Sure. I'll unlock the front door.'

Elodie closed the window and went back over to the security panel, buzzed open the street door of the studio. The sound of Lincoln's firm tread coming up to her floor sent her heart thumping.

Was he here to pull the plug on her label? In spite of threatening to withdraw his support the night she'd left, he hadn't done any such thing. She hadn't been game to read too much into it, but she was grateful for the extra time to get her business up and running without having to seek another sponsor.

She was standing by her work table when he came in, looking windswept and tired and drained but as gorgeous to her as ever.

'I suppose you're here about the money?' She kept her voice calm and controlled. No mixing emotions and business, right? That was her motto, taken straight from his hard-nosed businessman's playbook.

Lincoln came over to her and took her hands in his. 'I have never said this to anyone before, so hear me out. I love you. I've missed you so much—not just this last month but for the past seven years. I've filled my life with work and activity, but the one thing that was missing was you. I'm sorry it's taken me so long to realise what was there all the time. My love for you.'

Elodie stared at him in shock, her heart beating so hard and fast it was making her dizzy. 'You're not just saying it? You really love me?'

'I'm not just saying it. I'm feeling it in every part of my body. I ache for you. I feel incomplete without you in my life. Nothing fills the emptiness you left behind. You're my centre, my anchor, my one true love, and I beg you to come back to me and be my wife. And one day even the mother of my children, if that's what you want.'

Elodie stared at him for a moment, struck dumb by his emotional openness. He had never shown her his heart, never opened it fully to her the way he was doing now. He had always kept a bit of himself back, and it had made it hard for her to believe he would ever toss away his armour and let her in.

She threw her arms around his neck and squealed for joy. 'Oh, Lincoln, darling, of course I will. I love you so much. I've been so sad about leaving you, but I convinced myself you could never allow yourself to love me. But hearing you say it…it's just so wonderful. There are no words to describe how I feel right now, knowing you love me.'

Lincoln framed her face with his hands and gazed into her eyes. 'You were right about the way I conduct my relationships. It struck a chord when you said the loss of my biological mother at birth and then the sudden death of my adoptive mother had made me shut down the possibility of loving someone in a romantic sense. The threat of losing that kind of love was too daunting, too terrifying. I realise now I rushed our first relationship. I didn't give you time or your own space for growth within it. No wonder you ran away. But I promise not to do it this time. We'll be true equals, working together on everything. I want you by my side for the rest of my life.'

Elodie rose up on tiptoe to kiss him. 'I want you by my side too. You are the only man I've ever loved. I truly was dreading going on with my life without you. I was considering a life of celibacy. I couldn't bear the thought of anyone else touching me.'

Lincoln gathered her close, hugging her so tightly it almost took her breath away. 'I'm the same. I spent a month in New York thinking only of you. I ached for you every night and every morning.' There was a catch in his voice and then he continued, 'I have another apology to make.' He released her a little so he could meet her gaze once more. 'I'm sorry I didn't believe you about the engagement ring.'

Elodie's eyes rounded to the size of baubles. 'Morag told you?'

He gave a grim nod. 'Yes—although I blame myself for the way I insisted on her removing everything of yours from the house. I even cut her off when she tried to tell me a couple of times, refusing to allow her to say your name in my presence. But the thing I find so touching is that you didn't betray what she'd done to me once you found out.'

'You're not going to fire her, are you?'

'Only if you want me to.'

'No, I don't. I think she got it wrong, but she did what she thought was best for you. She didn't realise I loved you back then. She thought I was a star-struck gold-digger. And her keeping the ring hidden from you more or less proved it to you.'

Lincoln gave a rueful twist of his mouth. 'The thing is, I think on some level I never believed you loved me. I'm ashamed to say I quite liked you being a little star-struck and infatuated with me. It fed my ego and allowed me to railroad you into marriage. But of course, that didn't go to plan. And I'm glad now that it didn't. I think we both needed time to let go of our baggage and come back to each other as fully mature adults who want to spend the rest of their lives together.'

Elodie smiled and tenderly stroked his jaw. 'I promise to always be little star-struck by you if you promise to be star-struck by me.'

'I'll let you in on a little secret—I've always been a little star-struck by you.'

And he covered her mouth in a kiss that left her in no doubt of his enduring love and adoration.

EPILOGUE

Eighteen months later...

ELODIE LOOKED AT Lincoln, talking to Nina in the garden of their London home. He was smiling at something his mother said, and Nina's face was shining with love and happiness and, yes, even good health.

Nina's cancer had gone into remission, and so far things were tracking well. It was a miracle—one they were all so very grateful for. Elodie had grown increasingly close to Lincoln's biological mother, and had found Nina's support during her rising career as a designer invaluable. Her first show had been a phenomenal success, and she was feeling more fulfilled than she had ever dreamed possible.

And speaking of miracles...

Elodie's gaze drifted to her twin Elspeth, sitting beside her devoted husband, Mack, each of them holding in their arms a cute-as-a-button baby girl—identical twins called Maisie and Mackenzie. The besotted love on the new parents' faces said it all, and no one could have been happier for them than Elodie—especially since she and Lincoln had their own special news to share.

Lincoln came over to her and slipped an arm around her waist. 'Shall we tell them now, my love?'

'Oh, my God, you're pregnant?' Elspeth cried out in delighted joy. 'I just *knew* you were keeping a secret from me.'

Elodie's smile almost split her face in two. 'Yes— ten weeks. We wanted to wait until we were a little further along, but my tummy is already about to pop the zip on my jeans.'

Lincoln stroked a loving hand down the back of her head. 'We're expecting twins. Too early to know the sex.'

Nina didn't bother hiding the tracks of the tears pouring down her face. 'Oh, my darlings…you've made me the happiest person alive.'

Lincoln smiled down at Elodie, his expression so full of love it made her heart flutter. 'Our babies couldn't wish for a more beautiful and loving mother. And I couldn't wish for a more beautiful and loving wife.'

Elodie blinked back tears and grasped his hand, held it against her cheek. 'I love you.'

He bent down and placed a soft kiss to her lips. 'I love you too. Before, now and for ever.'

* * * * *

#3969 CINDERELLA'S BABY CONFESSION
by Julia James

Alys's unexpected letter confessing to the consequences of their one unforgettable night has ironhearted Nikos reconsidering his priorities. He'll bring Alys to his Greek villa, where he *will* claim his heir. By first unraveling the truth...and then her!

#3970 PREGNANT BY THE WRONG PRINCE
Pregnant Princesses
by Jackie Ashenden

Molded to be the perfect queen, Lia's sole rebellion was her night in Prince Rafael's powerful arms. She never dared dream of more. But now Rafael's stopping her arranged wedding—to claim her and the secret she carries!

#3971 STRANDED WITH HER GREEK HUSBAND
by Michelle Smart

Marooned on a Greek island with her estranged but gloriously attractive husband, Keren has nowhere to run. Not just from the tragedy that broke her and Yannis apart, but from the joy and passion she's tried—and failed—to forget...

#3972 RETURNING FOR HIS UNKNOWN SON
by Tara Pammi

Eight years after a plane crash left Christian with no memory of his convenient vows to Priya, he returns—and learns of his heir! To claim his family, he makes Priya an electrifying proposal: three months of living together...as man and wife.

#3973 ONE SNOWBOUND NEW YEAR'S NIGHT
by Dani Collins

Rebecca has one New Year's resolution: divorce Donovan Scott. Being snowbound at his mountain mansion isn't part of the plan. And what happens when it becomes clear the chemistry that led to their elopement is still very much alive?

#3974 VOWS ON THE VIRGIN'S TERMS
The Cinderella Sisters
by Clare Connelly

A four-week paper marriage to Luca to save her family from destitution seems like an impossible ask for innocent Olivia... Until he says yes! And then, on their honeymoon, the most challenging thing becomes resisting her irresistible new husband...

#3975 THE ITALIAN'S BARGAIN FOR HIS BRIDE
by Chantelle Shaw

By marrying heiress Paloma, self-made tycoon Daniele will help her protect her inheritance. In return, he'll gain the social standing he needs. Their vows are for show. The heat between them is definitely, maddeningly, *not*!

#3976 THE RULES OF THEIR RED-HOT REUNION
by Joss Wood

When Aisha married Pasco, she naively followed her heart. Not anymore! Back in the South African billionaire's world—as his business partner—she'll rewrite the terms of their relationship. Only, their reunion takes a dangerously scorching turn...

HPCNMRB1221

*Rebecca has one New Year's resolution: divorce
Donovan Scott. Being snowbound at his mountain
mansion isn't part of the plan. And what happens
when it becomes clear the chemistry that led to their
elopement is still very much alive?*

*Read on for a sneak preview of Dani Collins's
next story for Harlequin Presents,*
One Snowbound New Year's Night.

Van slid the door open and stepped inside only to have Becca
squeak and dance her feet, nearly dropping the groceries she'd
picked up.

"You knew I was here," he insisted. "That's why I woke you, so
you would know I was here and you wouldn't do that. I *live* here,"
he said for the millionth time, because she'd always been leaping
and screaming when he came around a corner.

"Did you? I never noticed," she grumbled, setting the bag on the
island and taking out the milk to put it in the fridge. "I was alone
here so often, I forgot I was married."

"*I* noticed that," he shot back with equal sarcasm.

They glared at each other. The civility they'd conjured in
those first minutes upstairs was completely abandoned—probably
because the sexual awareness they'd reawakened was still hissing
and weaving like a basket of cobras between them, threatening to
strike again.

Becca looked away first, thrusting the eggs into the fridge along
with the pair of rib eye steaks and the package of bacon.

She hated to be called cute and hated to be ogled, so Van tried
not to do either, but *come on*. She was curvy and sleepy and wearing
that cashmere like a second skin. She was shorter than average and
had always exercised in a very haphazard fashion, but nature had
gifted her with a delightfully feminine figure-eight symmetry. Her

ample breasts were high and firm over a narrow waist, then her hips flared into a gorgeous, equally firm and round ass. Her fine hair was a warm brown with sun-kissed tints, her mouth wide, and her dark brown eyes positively soulful.

When she smiled, she had a pair of dimples that he suddenly realized he hadn't seen in far too long.

"I don't have to be here right now," she said, slipping the coffee into the cupboard. "If you're going skiing tomorrow, I can come back while you're out."

"We're ringing in the New Year right here." He chucked his chin at the windows that climbed all the way to the peak of the vaulted ceiling. Beyond the glass, the frozen lake was impossible to see through the thick and steady flakes. A gray-blue dusk was closing in.

"You have four-wheel drive, don't you?" Her hair bobbled in its knot, starting to fall as she snapped her head around. She fixed her hair as she looked back at him, arms moving with the mysterious grace of a spider spinning her web. "How did you get here?"

"Weather reports don't apply to me," he replied with self-deprecation. "Gravity got me down the driveway and I won't get back up until I can start the quad and attach the plow blade." He scratched beneath his chin, noted her betrayed glare at the windows.

Believe me, sweetheart. I'm not any happier than you are.

He thought it, but immediately wondered if he was being completely honest with himself.

"How was the road?" She fetched her phone from her purse, distracting him as she sashayed back from where it hung under her coat. "I caught a rideshare to the top of the driveway and walked down. I can meet one at the top to get back to my hotel."

"Plows will be busy doing the main roads. And it's New Year's Eve," he reminded her.

"So what am I supposed to do? Stay here? All night? With *you*?"

"Happy New Year," he said with a mocking smile.

Don't miss
One Snowbound New Year's Night.
Available January 2022 wherever
Harlequin Presents books and ebooks are sold.

Harlequin.com

Copyright © 2021 by Dani Collins

HPEXP1221